THE COLONEL'S CLAY

THE COLONEL'S CLAY

Library of Congress Control Number: 2020913684
ISBN: 978-0-9863992-4-4

Writers Bloc
Jonesboro, Arkansas

THE COLONEL'S CLAY

A NOVEL BY

VAN HAWKINS

ALSO BY VAN HAWKINS

Hampton and Newport News
A look at two historic Virginia towns, 1975

Dorothy and the Shipbuilders of Newport News
The story of an iconic American shipyard, 1976

The Historic Triangle
How Jamestown, Williamsburg, and Yorktown
made American history, 1980

Plowing New Ground
The Southern Tenant Farmers Union
and its place in Delta History, 2007

Duty Bound
The Hyatt brothers and Confederates
of the Third Arkansas Infantry Regiment, 2011

Horizons
A novel about growing up in a small southern town
in the 1950s and 1960s, 2012

Smoke Up the River
Steamboats and the Arkansas Delta, *2016*

Moaning Low: From Slavery to Peonage
Involuntary Servitude in the Arkansas Delta, 2019

A New Deal in Dyess:
The Depression Era Agricultural Resettlement Colony
in Arkansas, 2020

ABOUT THE AUTHOR

Van Hawkins grew up in a farming family in the Missouri Bootheel. He has a degree in literature from the University of Missouri, as well as master's degrees in pastoral counseling from Loyola University in New Orleans, and heritage studies from Arkansas State University.

Van has worked as a newspaper reporter and editor and as an entertainment magazine feature writer. His books are written for general audiences on topics related to southern history. Van and his wife, Ruth, reside in Jonesboro, Arkansas.

For Ruth,
who has lived with this book
for a long time

WHERE MANY THINGS ARE HIDDEN

1

Though only 15, Jesse Brody Morrisey looked much older. A large and muscular boy, he had brown eyes set in a long, angular face dotted with a few freckles and capped by light brown hair. His family lived in a small plank house along the Illinois River at Beardstown, where his father worked as a boatbuilder. The boy considered school a waste of time after learning to read, write, and do sums. So he skipped class whenever possible and walked along the cracked, charcoal gray piers where he stared wistfully at boats coming and going. Jesse longed to be on a departing steamer and distance himself from a mean father who beat his mother often and a priest who would not grant her a divorce because it violated church rules made by old white men in Rome. Though only 16 at the time, Jesse's sister, a pretty girl with curly auburn hair, took up with an older man to get away.

Jesse got away when *Buckeye State* made preparations to depart on a hot July morning. From an ancient wood pier the boy watched deck hands standing on a groaning gangplank loading crates from a wharf. They were behind schedule because one man sprained his back and could no longer hold a place in the line. The injured man sat on a rough-hewn stack of wood staves on the wharf and argued with a bulky first mate with curly blond hair and a pockmarked face who was supervising the loading. Jesse heard the injured man complain to the first mate. "No suh, that ain't right. You holdin' out all my money ain't right. No suh, it ain't right. I got babes to feed. I got to have me some money." His complaints caused a flicker of doubt among the remaining stevedores who wondered if the injured man would be paid a full wage, the same as them, despite not having worked as long. The mate sensed a brewing controversy and decided to end it. "Jimmy," he said to the injured man, "I'm going to pay you a half wage because the deal was you had to finish to get paid anything. But since you got hurt and didn't shirk, I'll pay you that much if you shut up so we can get on with it. I don't need a boy telling me how to handle a loading crew. If you keep mouthing off you'll get nothing. Now shut your ugly face."

Jimmy nodded slowly. "That's all right. We all right then." He shifted his weight along the staves and shook his head. "Dadgummit. Now I got a splinter in my ass. A big

4

one." He reached back and rubbed the sore spot beneath his dirty cotton pants while his face filled with a frown. "Yessir. Now I got a big splinter in my ass. I don't know what I'm gonna do about that. No, sir."

Jesse had been standing at the edge of the pier listening, and the mate turned to him. "What do you want?"

"I want to help load the steamer."

The mate gave him a brief looking over. "Get in the line, but if you drop anything I'll throw you head first into that stinking water." Jesse looked down at a ribbon of dirty foam that bordered the pier's base and determined to avoid it. The boy held his own for a while among the strong black men despite aches and near exhaustion. When the chief steward walked onto the main deck to check progress he saw Jesse struggling to hold his place in line.

The short, astonishingly thin steward wore a tight-fitting black suit and had straightened, coal black hair roached back and stuck to his scalp with bear grease. The man had a high-pitched voice and sounded like a girl. "Who is that boy?" he asked the first mate.

"He's a come-along."

"Any good?"

"He's about played out, but game enough."

The chief steward walked up to Jesse and came to the point. "I need a cabin boy for four dollars a month. You get free eats, clean uniforms, and a pallet to sleep on. You want the job?"

"Yes, sir," Jesse replied without weighing the consequences.

"Go home and get your belongings and kiss your mama goodbye. Ask for me when you get back. I'm Julian."

"Don't have anything to get, and my mama is dead." Jesse lied, thinking that it might simplify things if he had no family to speak of.

"Then finish up here and find me. I'll be on the hurricane deck."

Jesse waited until the chief steward walked back into the passageway and disappeared in the shadows. He turned to the mate. "Sir, what is a hurricane deck?" Jesse asked as he heaved a tub of lard to the next man in line.

"The hurricane deck is on top, above the texas deck, boiler deck, and main deck. You're on the main deck now."

Jesse's question caused him to slow down the line, and the other loaders began to stare. "How do I get there?"

This question irritated the first mate, but he answered it anyhow. "You climb the aft ladder until you get to the top

6

deck." He stared at Jesse's blank eyes and continued. "The aft ladder is at the back of the steamer. It is the plain one, not the fancy one. Never take the fancy stairs. That is for cabin passengers. Now you might as well go on up there. All you're doing here is slowing down the line. We're almost finished anyhow, and I don't want the chief steward complaining to me. I'll pay you six bits next time I see you."

Jesse found the hurricane deck and Julian observing two young men swabbing water puddles standing in shallow dips in the rubbed raw wood deck. He looked at Jesse carefully. "Come along now. We have to get you into some different clothes before you go to work." The different clothes amounted to clean privy drawers, black pants, a heavily starched white shirt, black vest, and black bow tie. The boy quickly found out the nature of his unenviable job. It amounted to fetching and carrying, running errands, and tending to cabin passengers' orders. Julian explained the guiding principle governing cabin boy behavior. "You never see anything you are not supposed to see. If something seems amiss you come to me. You never, and I mean never, approach a cabin passenger with anything but a smile on your face and sweetness in your heart. You are available all day and all night. You will sleep on a mat in an area of the cabin where your assigned staterooms are located."

After the chief steward pointed to Jesse's sleeping space he walked the boy around the cabin. "To clear up what is often misunderstood by new hires, the cabin is the large area where staterooms are located. It does not refer to an individual room. Cabins offer accommodations and facilities for passengers and crew. As you can see, it consists of a long and narrow space flanked on each side by a row of staterooms. On either side in line with staterooms are the clerk's office and the bar. The captain's quarters and those of the pilots are located in the cabin's forward area. Washrooms, the barbershop, nursery, pantry, kitchen, and other service rooms are on either side of the cabin."

Jesse followed Julian and attempted to memorize his information. The chief steward pointed to a rear section of the cabin and continued. "The ladies cabin is located at the rear of the boiler deck, as far as possible from heat and noise generated by steamboat engines. Partitions separate rooms assigned to women to maintain their modesty. They enjoy elegant accommodations. Their staterooms usually have small windows for light and ventilation. Men are allowed in the ladies cabin only during daylight hours. However, some large staterooms serve entire families, including husbands. Breakfast is served from 7 to 9 a.m. Lunch at 1 p.m. And dinner at 6 p.m. Colored chambermaids tidy up cabins during meals and common areas throughout the day. They all wear long cotton dresses and aprons.

"Just before daylight you will go to the galley and quickly eat breakfast, then change into clean, freshly pressed clothes in the laundry room. Though it is highly unlikely, should a cabin passenger ring for service at daylight you will forget breakfast and change clothes immediately. The other boys will fill you in on the rest." The rest included an odious chore that sometimes made Jesse sick. At dawn the cabin boys carried out chamber pots from rooms and dumped their human waste into the river from a designated place on the vessel's stern. They then rinsed out the pots with river water and returned them to staterooms. Jesse sometimes threw up when a breeze blew the stench into his face. Following this chore, cabin boys took what they called a whore's bath with harsh lye soap and water then returned to their stations.

When the steamer docked, Julian assigned porters to escort boarding cabin passengers to their staterooms. On those occasions Jesse watched from the boiler deck an amazing collection of people---businessmen wearing conservative suits and worried expressions; handsome young men with practiced smiles in black formal wear looking for an heiress; rough and tumble boatmen; Quakers in their peculiar garbs; soldiers in uniform; backwoodsmen wearing leather shirts and pants who avoided bathing; poor midwestern farmers with wives in faded Mother Hubbard dresses, and planters in neatly pressed linen suits. Taken all together, the lines of bustling people reminded Jesse of a shifting rainbow.

After several weeks of observing life on the Upper Mississippi he gained an opportunity for advancement. Two food servers stole several Smithfield hams, stuffed them in poke sacks and jumped off the main deck guard into shoe-top mud. Julian woke Jesse just before daylight. "Stow your mat and meet me in the galley."

"What about the stuff I got to do?"

"I'll spread it around the rest of them. Now do what you're told."

Jesse did what he was told and found Julian in the galley going over a morning menu with his head chef. The perplexed boy stood aside and watched until they finished and Julian turned to him. "Get down to the laundry and put on a food service uniform and meet me in the cabin." The uniform consisted of a black tuxedo, a little too small for him, but a seamstress said she would fit out a larger one for the next day. When Jesse walked into the cabin he saw servers setting up a long table to feed the first round of guests. Julian pulled a boy toward Jesse. "This is Maxwell. You will assist him and do exactly what he says. He will help me make up for the two thieves who jumped overboard, may they rot in hell with their first-born child."

Jesse saw pretty fast how the system worked. Julian walked down one side of the table followed by several waiters. He wrote down orders by numbers on individual tickets and handed three tickets to each server. They rushed to the kitchen to fetch dishes noted on their slips and deliver them to the correct patrons. During this process the diners treated servers with a chilly politeness or mild contempt. Maxwell did the same on his side of the table with Jesse the last waiter in line. Maxwell took the last five slips and had Jesse follow him. As they loaded dishes on trays to match orders, Maxwell gave Jesse a tray and simple instructions. "Serve people from their left side. If you do something wrong, say I beg your pardon, and make it right. If you make a mess I'll help you clean it up, but don't make a mess. As soon as we finish here I have to go with Julian to the staterooms and take orders from people who want to eat in their rooms. A lot of women do that because they don't want to gussy up this early in the day."

Fortunately, Jesse did not make a mess and offered to assist Maxwell with cabin orders. Jesse saw relief in his expression and followed Maxwell to the cabin. This service proved to be easier since they hauled orders on a cart. Julian observed Jesse's manner and how fast he learned, which confirmed the chief steward's decision to assign him an available position. After food deliveries Jesse approached Maxwell with a question. "What do we do now?"

"We clear the table. When cabin passengers finish they put their trays outside the door. We pick them up next. Just do what I do."

The noon meal displayed more formality. After servers filled the table with dishes inspected by Julian he went to the ladies cabin and announced service. Elegantly attired women took their places at the upper end of the long table. A bell then gave notice that gentlemen should seat themselves at the lower end. Servers stood behind diners at decent intervals to deliver drinks and bring special items when requested. All the while, Julian carefully observed the goings on like a falcon looking for prey and moved to assist when necessary. Jesse noticed that the gentlemen and ladies hardly said a word to each other during their meal. Many men excused themselves when done eating and headed to the bar. Ladies returned to their staterooms to freshen up, as they put it. Then came the captain and other ship officers. When they finished, waiters cleared plates, many with uneaten food on them. As Jesse started to scrape scraps into a trash can Maxwell stopped him. "Put it on that table over there with all the rest. The chief steward gives us a couple of minutes to eat scraps before our chores." Jesse learned that by custom, servers could only eat food on plates they cleared, which explained why experienced boys picked up plates with the most food on them.

After finishing his scraps, Jesse followed Maxwell to a deck guard outside the cabin for fresh air and started a conversation. He learned that Maxwell Hess had immigrated with his family from Munich, Germany, to St.

Louis. Though revealing a slight German accent, his vocabulary exceeded Jesse's by a long shot thanks to a completed Catholic school education. Plus, he was several years older and appeared to have learned demeanor and personal habits by observing cabin passengers. "I want to be a pilot," Maxwell told him. "I plan to save enough money to pay a pilot to apprentice me. That's the fastest way to do it."

He paused, thinking about something unsaid, and Jesse spoke up. "Why do you want to be a pilot?"

Maxwell scratched his head and shrugged. "The money is good. Some of them make $100 per month, as much as captains. They get to travel a lot and see different people and places. I watched steamers from piers in St. Louis all the time and always wanted to be a pilot. I want to know all they know and have people trusting me while their steamer barrels down the river on a pitch-black night. I guess I just always wanted to be one."

When *Buckeye State* reached the Mississippi River several weeks later on another of its many trips, Jesse stood on the main deck guard during one of his few breaks. He became fascinated with how the scenery was changing, both along the river and on it. Land grew flatter and the soil darker on much of the east side. High ground along the shore fought to hold the river in check, but in some places the river won, and the soil caved in, taking trees and brush with it. They often formed thick reefs, dangerous barriers that could rip open a steamer's thin skin.

Thanks to Hess and his preparations to become a pilot, Jesse learned many of the river's tricks and threats. Bendways were lateral bends of the river created through erosion of banks on the outside of curves and sediment deposits inside curves. Undercurrents alongside a main flow of water formed eddies. Snags became sawyers when they made an up and down motion in the water. Ripples and shoals signaled where sandbars came in quick succession. Flumes were places where water shot through narrow channels, and its speed threatened to overcome a pilot's skills. Sidewheelers were faster and more maneuverable, and engines located next to paddles reduced vibration and passenger complaints. However, new sternwheeler designs during the late 1870s solved many vibration problems and made them increasingly popular.

2

Modest steamers plying routes in the Upper Mississippi, said to start in Cairo, Illinois, gave way to large, ornate steamboats in the Lower Mississippi, which ended at the Gulf of Mexico. Called floating palaces, they stood high and proud in the water. Jesse decided that he wanted to be on one, and he reached that decision without much consideration. After roustabouts tied up at a Memphis pier he walked away with his belongings in a bag. Jesse strolled along piers and stared at magnificent vessels lined up like rows of shiny white teeth. He knew from shipboard gossip that most steamers always needed help due to a continuous turnover of personnel. On a Monday afternoon in a light drizzle he saw *Mary Bell*, a white gingerbread masterpiece. Jesse walked over a gangway onto its main deck until the first mate stopped him. The man had immense muscles, skin burned brown by the sun, long black hair tied in a ponytail, and a dense Irish brogue. "What's with you boy?"

"I'm looking for work."

"What sort of work are you good for?"

"I've been a waiter on *Buckeye State* for a few weeks. I want to get on a better boat."

"Any boat would be better than that one," the first mate said sarcastically. "You get let go?"

"No sir."

The mate eyed him carefully before yelling into a nearby passageway. "Mackey, come take the watch while I go topside." Another large man, shirtless, covered with sweat and gaudy tattoos, walked out of the darkness and blinked repeatedly to regain his vision.

The first mate turned to Jesse. "You stay here until I get back. I'll check with the chief steward to see if he needs some help."

A few minutes later the portly chief steward pranced out of the passageway. Monsieur Roget had a round, red face squatting on two rolls of fat around his neck. He sculpted his hair into a cone that resembled a small volcano yet to erupt, and his French accent sometimes made him difficult to understand. Jesse learned later that his accent had a New Jersey quality. Monsieur's massive belly stretched out his tuxedo coat almost to the breaking point, and Jesse thought that if you stuck a pin in his stomach his guts would explode in every direction and seriously injure nearby people. After a few questions about details of food service, which Jesse answered correctly, the steward hired him. "Thank you, sir," the new hire said.

"You must call me Monsieur at all times. Nothing else will do."

Jesse paused while following the chief steward and glanced at a few of the dishes included in an extensive menu displayed on an ornate bulkhead near the cabin entrance. Monsieur's insistence on using the French language when possible made matters difficult. Entrees included boiled redfish maître d'hotel, roast beef with caper sauce, calves feet a la Pauceline, filets of chicken with truffles, poitrine d'agneau, la reine d'agneau, avec pots vertis, and many others.

The chief steward noticed his consternation. "Come along now. There will be time for admiration later."

"Yes, Monsieur."

"Keep in mind that if you don't behave properly and make your manners at all times I'll have the first mate put you off at the next landing."

"You can count on me."

"Very well, we shall see."

Though scheduled to get underway the next day, boiler problems caused a delay in the luxurious steamer's departure. This gave Jesse more time to learn about the vessel. When Captain J. Frank Hicks launched *Mary Bell,* a *St. Louis Times* declared it "Queen of the Mississippi." An article from the *Louisville Courier-Journal* posted in the enormous cabin praised the steamer as well: its handsome stairs, elegant staterooms, extensive promenades, silver-plated tableware, and a glossy white cabin with magnificent chandeliers. The newspaper said that taken as a whole, *"Mary Bell* is the most complete steamboat" on the Mississippi.

After the luxurious steamboat headed downriver Jesse sometimes between chores had time to stand on the hurricane deck and watch people ashore admiring the vessel. Haggard dirt farmers walked along pig paths to the river's edge after hearing a steamer's whistle or spotting smoke up the river. They stared at the boat and waved to passengers but received no acknowledgement. These country folks were unaware that Paris was only 100 yards away. French dancers and chefs created a view of life beyond the imagination of those ashore. During Sunday afternoons, a brass band often performed on the texas deck and attracted crowds at small landings. Black families dressed in their clean and starched church clothes came to listen to the music and dance. Southern steamboat patrons, seeking to legitimize their horrific treatment of them, laughed and pointed to the display as proof of an inferiority that had to be guided by wiser heads.

During his ramblings Jesse saw several men dressed alike in fancy clothes. They wore black coats and trousers, black boots, white shirts cut low with frills, gaudy vests with pearl buttons, and diamond rings on at least two fingers. They had gold pocket watches in their vests attached to long gold chains looped around their necks and draped across the front of their shirts. These men appeared to enjoy playing cards and seemed uncommonly lucky. A cabin boy told Jesse what they did and to stay away from them. After several weeks aboard, while traveling south out of Vicksburg, Jesse saw the Colonel in a barbershop. The elderly gentleman was immaculately dressed in a conservative gray suit without adornments of any sort. His handsome face and graying hair reminded Jesse of a kindly grandfather. The boy recalled seeing him at the cabin table during meals and sometimes served the Colonel. In the barbershop Jesse observed him playing three-card monte. The Colonel showed players a queen of hearts and two other cards. He then shuffled all three face down. A player attempted to pick the lady and pocket the wager. While Jesse watched, several men succeeded and won small bets. Rattlesnake Jack, who Jesse later learned was secretly in cahoots with the Colonel, limped into the room faking a knee injury and complained of losses in a poker game. "Well," the Colonel said, "We at this table are just passing time enjoying a game on the square."

"Then let me bet you $100 that I can pick the winner," Jack said. He won and bet $500 on the next draw. He won that too. As the Colonel bent over to pick up a card that hit the floor in a faked shuffling error, Jack put a tiny crease in the edge of a winning card and winked at three suckers standing beside him. When the Colonel looked up, Jack raised the stakes to $1,000. With bulging pockets from cotton sales, three planters saw a sure thing and placed their bets.

Jesse saw the same sure thing and pulled out nine dollars, his life's savings. "I want to bet this."

The Colonel looked at him casually. "Lad, take your money and be gone. I don't make bets with children."

"I'm not a child, and this is all the money I got in the world," Jesse replied, irritated that his grip on this sure thing was slipping away.

"Son, give me your money," a planter said. He turned to the Colonel. "Add this to my bet, and I'll settle up with the boy."

The Colonel nodded after a moment's reflection. "Very well." He moved the cards around quickly until the winning card rested hidden in his palm and the three down cards all had tiny creases. During this deal Jack had a coughing fit that distracted the suckers. A planter looked at the three cards, hesitated, gulped, and guessed at their sure thing winner. When the card turned over his face went snow white. "Well, well," he stammered. "I'll be."

Jack let out a loud moan like he had been gut shot that drew the planters' attention for a moment, which allowed the Colonel to switch the winner from his hand to the table and palm a tabled card. It went so smooth that no one saw it. He then turned over the two cards, and there was the sure thing winner. A distraught Jesse stepped back from the table slowly and silently while Jack continued to moan. "Oooh. How am I gonna tell my wife that I lost all of her mother's homestead money." This made planter losses less onerous since they didn't have to tell their wives that story.

After this shock their game broke up, and a sad Jesse walked toward the cabin door until the Colonel called out. "Lad, join me on the deck." He walked out with Jesse close behind. They sat down in deck chairs near the guard far from other passengers. Jesse began to fidget, worrying about the chief steward seeing him relaxing among passengers. The Colonel read him like he read everyone, quick and true. "Don't worry, the crew will not bother you. The first thing I do after coming aboard a steamer is to show my appreciation to certain men in control of matters. The chief steward is one of them." His soft, soothing voice calmed Jesse somewhat, and the Colonel peeled off five dollars from a thick gambler's roll and handed it to the boy. "I will only give you part of your loss so that you will feel some pain over a bad decision."

"I should have known better. Mama told me never to play games of chance."

"That was not a game of chance. You had no chance at all. My luck is always the residue of design."

Jesse's brow formed a furrow. "What do you mean?"

"All in good time, when you are ready. That brings me to the purpose of our chat. I would like to hire you as my assistant, in training, of course. Should I not be pleased with your work I will dismiss you and pay the balance of what I owe you."

"Training for what?"

"To assist me in my endeavors."

"Do I get paid?"

"Of course. I will double your current salary and give you a small percentage of what I earn with your assistance. I will pay all of your expenses. This is a generous offer."

"Do I have to do anything illegal?"

"Though it does not appear to be, that is a complicated question. But I can assure you that you will never suffer from legal repercussions due to your association with me. Most of your time will be spent furthering your education." The Colonel paused and smiled. "Sporting men have always been part of life, even from ancient cultures. The Greeks and Romans played games with risk, kings and queens as well. Descartes and Montaigne enjoyed a toss. Even moralists found pleasure in gaming. John Wesley, founder of the Methodist religion, played cards.

Jesse hesitated, suppressing many questions. "I never heard of those men. I don't know what to say. I don't know what you want me to do." He paused. "What will the chief steward say. He might throw me off the boat."

"That will not happen. I made arrangements with him should you agree, and he is satisfied."

Though filled with doubts and not sure why, Jesse accepted.

"Good," the Colonel said. "At ten in the morning come to my stateroom, and we shall begin your tutelage. Be prompt. You must always be prompt. You should continue to sleep where you are until I can arrange a private room. If I move you into my cabin some will think you are a fancy boy. We cannot have that. I will arrange matters with the ship's officers."

After this conversation Jesse asked an older boy who waited tables with him what fancy boy meant. The reply caused him to blush cherry red and say, "Oh my goodness."

3

The apprentice soon learned why the Colonel recruited him. His mentor's previous young capper fell in love with a toothless whore on a Natchez wharfboat and ran off with her. Rattlesnake Jack had about run his course as well. He took his name after claiming to have been bitten by a rattler in west Texas and survived, but the snake died. Jack chewed tobacco all the time, and during his last train trip capping for the Colonel he caused a stir. When Jack opened a window beside his coach seat to spit, a spirited matron sitting behind him by an open window squealed like a hog stuck in a gate when a glob splattered between her eyes. The woman's husband licked his handkerchief and tried to wash it off, but with little success. He then left his seat, walked up to Jack, and challenged him to a duel. This was an odd gesture since that practice largely disappeared during the so-called war of northern aggression, when most southern hot bloods decided to kill Yankees instead of each other. A conductor walked up in time to stop talk of armed satisfaction and made Jack ride in the baggage car with a spit cup. This did not please the Colonel. It called too much attention to Jack, and unwelcome attention did not suit those in the Colonel's trade.

On the morning of their first tutorial, after learning of Jack's deteriorating relationship with the Colonel, Jesse asked about Jack's future and received a blunt answer. "He has no future with me. Jack has honed useful skills for capping, and it pains me to speak ill of the man. But when you study him carefully Jack appears to be an idiot, and I fear he is." The Colonel paused. "Regardless, the useful life of a capper is limited. Many posh Delta travelers take steamers frequently, and they expect to see sporting men. But if they identify a capper and associate him with a particular player one can hardly expect them to sit down with the two for an evening of sport. So I am always on the lookout for new associates. Jack and I must part ways with a sad smile." The Colonel's tone shifted. "Keep in mind that you should always employ a capper. A good one can divert attention at the right time and read the attitude of marks, if they will kick and how hard."

"Why did you pick me? You never saw me before."

"On the contrary. I have watched you carefully for a good while. I observed your attitude around people of means and your talent for imitation. And, I should add, your hands. You have large hands and long fingers. They are an important tool in our trade." The boy would learn this when he practiced holding one deck in the palm of his hand while cutting another man's deal. He became good enough, but good enough was never good enough for the Colonel. It fell short of perfection.

Meanwhile, Jesse studied the stateroom, the largest he had ever seen on a steamboat. One open trunk appeared to be filled with books. Polished burled wood lined its bulkhead. The cabin had elegant furniture with a four-poster bed and a colorful Oriental carpet, though the boy had no idea what to call it. "This is a nice room."

"Yes it is," the Colonel replied. "Eventually you will have one like it. So we should begin preparations."

"What is your name?" Jesse asked.

"Let us not worry about that. Always call me Colonel. That will do."

The Colonel then began the boy's classes. Jesse learned that he must be prepared to assume three capper identities. One, a Texas rancher's son named Clem, an ignorant cowboy with pockets full of money after selling cattle in Kansas City. In the second, a young priest carrying his church's building funds. And third, the oldest son of a wealthy South Carolina planter family. The Colonel looked for marks every day, but usually did not set up a game until late afternoon when many male cabin passengers had reached a state of near drunkenness to outright drunkenness. So Jesse's education took place each morning and early afternoon for several hours. The boy practiced assuming each of the three identities quickly and surely and found his mentor unrelenting on matters of language and accents. Jesse had to learn advanced math in order to compute odds quickly if necessary. One of the Colonel's initial observations surprised him. "Lad, your grammar is sometimes deficient. Learn to talk the way I do but avoid large words for the time being. You would be taken for a poseur, a French word that you will find useful some day. We will work on that language along with your Latin."

"Latin! Why do I have to learn Latin?"

"Remember that you are a priest. Besides, every gentleman should be familiar with that language. Now do as you are told unless you want to resign."

"No, sir. I'm not a quitter."

"Then trust me. I know what is best for you, and you do not. The Colonel used three distinct American dialects: A deep South drawl as thick as fleas on a blue tick hound, clipped pronunciations of a midwestern businessman, and the cultivated speech of a Boston brahmin.

During the first weeks of his employment, Jesse observed the Colonel in action from a distance in the cabin and barbershop, but never in the bar. He learned how the Colonel picked marks and set them up. Jesse noted that the Colonel almost always selected suckers who would cheat him if given the opportunity or men whose greed outran their judgment. Somehow he spotted them every time and seemed to be able to see around corners. Jesse witnessed his powers of observation during a draw poker game on the square. A spotter for the Colonel's opponent had a toothpick in his mouth and stood to the Colonel's left. After he was outplayed several hands in a row the Colonel began to follow movements of the man's toothpick. Each time the Colonel had two pair or better the spotter took the toothpick out of his mouth. When the Colonel had a poor hand the toothpick went back in. After another losing hand the Colonel opened his coat to reveal Betsy, his Colt pistol, and turned to the spotter. "If you do not walk away you will not need that toothpick. Every tooth in your head will be broken." The spotter glanced at the gun and backed away slowly without uttering a denial. The Colonel returned to the game after having the bartender bring a cold deck and stitched up the grifter.

On that trip the Dripper capped for the Colonel. The name developed due to the man's urinary problems. Jesse once asked the Colonel why all cappers have strange nicknames.

The Colonel shrugged. "That is an excellent question. I have been puzzled by that since I began my river travels. No one seems to know how it started, so I have accepted it like everyone else." The Colonel knew the answers to almost everything else that Jesse asked. The sharper's edge, the Colonel advised, came from a variety of tools and knowledge. "You must quickly master the terminology and techniques necessary for success in our line of work. Professional players call themselves sporting men, but the public calls them slickers and sharpers. They run brace games, never on the square. You must recognize them immediately and never join a game controlled by one. That is a common courtesy. The targets of sporting men are most often said to be marks or punters. Cappers help set up marks and rig games. Kickers are losers who complain. Laying a bottom stock means dealing from the bottom of a deck. Called advantage tools, poker rings fitted with needle points make tiny indentations to read. Bribed bartenders hold reader decks and send them to a table when losers call for a cold deck. Some sporting men mark decks with a stripper. It shaves tiny slivers off cards in a deck, always high ones. A sporting man deals those to his hand for a big edge. Monte operators use three cards called tickets, often two aces and a queen. The dealer lays them face down, quickly shifts them about, and bets a punter to turn over the lady. But when the time comes to pick the lady she is palmed and not on the table. A professional's hands might be quicker than a sucker's eyes, but with a capper drawing attention away from the table at the right moment his hands do not have to be." The Colonel began to teach these and other valuable lessons to his protégé with this admonition. "Never let an opponent know your true strength. Remember that real power should be hidden until the holder decides to reveal it. If an opponent fails to perceive it early on, he has made a serious mistake."

Jesse especially enjoyed afternoons sitting on a deck chair beside the Colonel who lectured on steamboat history, displaying an elephantine memory. One day his mentor talked at great length about early years on the river, rarely pausing. "In the old days river traffic came and went mostly on flatboats and keelboats. The trip downstream benefitted from the current. But passage from New Orleans north to Louisville, Kentucky, for example, might take six months, since men who poled a craft had to push against strong currents. They typically came south with pork, flour, whiskey, tobacco from Kentucky, and cotton from the Delta." The Colonel stopped briefly. "If this is to be your place and people, you should know everything about them."

A server came out with coffee in a silver pot and offered to pour the Colonel's favorite, a strong chicory variety from Café Du Monde in New Orleans. "Thank you," he told the waiter. Jesse noticed early on that the Colonel always thanked those who served him, no matter their station in life. Most cabin guests treated service help poorly, berating them over the slightest slip up. Now Jesse also said thank you to those who served him. The boy also learned to stand when approached by a lady or gentleman. A gentleman should remain standing until they took their seats, the Colonel stressed. "At least in matters of social graces, southern ways are the best ways." The Colonel hesitated. "In other matters, the South has much cruelty to answer for."

Jesse already knew the Colonel's views about abuse of black people, so the boy avoided that subject. "When did steamers take over southern rivers?"

"When the steamboat *New Orleans* departed Pittsburgh in 1811 and headed for the port of New Orleans. It succeeded, despite having been threatened by massive earthquakes in southern Missouri. That vessel and others soon developed trade routes along the Lower Mississippi and turned steamboat travel and shipping into a major industry."

"I heard you say once that the Civil War destroyed river commerce."

The Colonel reflected for a moment. "The war caused a great many dislocations. After the Federals took Vicksburg their ironclads blocked the river. Cotton shipping practically ended, reducing ports like New Orleans to a shell. Union armies destroyed plantations along rivers and plundered their assets. It became what Sherman called total war."

When the Colonel halted, Jesse took a chance. "Did you fight in the war?"

"That is a private matter," he replied and ended the session.

The Colonel stressed Lower Mississippi history because of how it formed the habits and attitudes of many southern punters. They fancied themselves astute gamblers, and their arrogance made them easy marks for sharpers. Most midwestern farmers and businessmen lacked their conceit. Jesse learned how to recognize differences between the two and how to set them up. After a couple of months working on card skills Jesse became partial to faro, in which bettors wagered on the top card of a dealer's pack. The Colonel approved of the boy's progress. "Since you are becoming proficient in that game, we will provide time for British literature. Let us start with Dickens." Though Jesse did not like the idea, he accepted it since the Colonel would ignore his objections.

Still, Jesse frowned. "You are wasting your time with childish pique, so set it aside," the Colonel responded. "I will question you extensively after you finish, so do not try to bluff me. As you have learned while playing stud poker with me, your facial tells make you hopeless at bluffing. But that is for another time."

"I don't know what you see that gives me away."

"That is your problem, and I will not solve it for you. You should spend more time in front of a mirror learning the formation of misleading expressions for certain situations."

"I don't want to make you mad, but when do I get to do something instead of watching you take down marks?"

"You are not ready yet, even though you think you are. At this point you might make a mistake that puts you in physical jeopardy or subject to being blacklisted by steamboat captains. Both can be disastrous in their own way."

During a trip south on *Eclipse,* Jesse encountered an unusual disaster. The steamer docked at Natchez, but no passengers or freight rested on the pier. Instead, a town constable waited there. He called for the captain to come ashore, and they met briefly before the skipper returned to his vessel. Word came from ship's officers that talk of yellow fever in New Orleans had come upriver and that *Eclipse* would remain at Natchez until more could be learned about the report.

This led the Colonel and his protégé to lounge in empty deck chairs along the starboard guard, where the Colonel told him about the fate of a steamer, *John Porter,* due to a disaster during an 1878 epidemic. "After departing New Orleans, several of its crew became ill, and ports would not allow the vessel to tie up. But machinery problems forced it to shore about three miles from Gallapolis, Ohio. By then 23 of its 31-man crew were dead, and the fever spread to Gallapolis. Angry authorities burned the barges towed by *Porter* and fumigated the vessel."

"What happened to the steamer?"

"Captain John Porter renamed it *Sidney Dillon,* made several changes in its appearance, and sold the boat. But it burned soon thereafter in mysterious circumstances."

After two days Jesse got cabin fever and decided to go ashore, which did not please the Colonel. "Natchez is a hell with base amusements," he told Jesse. "It is wretched real estate infested with robbers and cutthroats, and there are houses along the river where people disappear forever. Young men are lured inside and murdered. Their bodies are stripped and dropped into the water. If you must go, take Cannon Ball Charley with you and be exceptionally careful." Jesse agreed and convinced Charley to go with him. The tall, muscular capper had a head shaped like a cannon ball, hence his name.

An area called Natchez Under the Hill extended below a bluff and ran along the Mississippi River. A dirt street went from Ray's store to an upper wharfboat. A path from a lower wharfboat to South and Reynolds streets enabled passengers to pass to and from steamers. Shabby little grog shops filled several muddy streets, and quadroon women in gay cotton dresses served broiled catfish on rough wood counters infested with flies. Boisterous voices and the smell of human waste filled the air. Shortly after they came ashore Jesse saw a man sitting on a wood plank walkway with his back against a plaster wall. A bright red ribbon of blood ran down his white face. When Jesse paused, Charley pushed him past the man. "Let him be. He's done for. The boys here will run a knife through you for a half dollar."

They first stopped at a notorious beer garden beneath the upper bluffs. Flambeaux flickered in a huge, vine-covered pavilion, and strumpets danced to the time of tinkling tambourines. Cockatoos flew above the crowd, occasionally emptying their bowels on customers too drunk to dodge. Jesse and Charley left before it was their turn.

"I heard about Madam Aivoges's house, and it's supposed to be fancy," Charley said. The brick building stood out among a row of tawdry shebangs, and a doorman looked them over before ushering the two into an attractive parlor. They ordered a small glass of gin for a dollar and looked around. A whore immediately sidled up to them. "Would you handsome gents buy me a drink?

"Yes we will," Charley replied. "What's your pleasure?"

"A fine white wine if you please."

A waiter brought it over without being asked, and Jesse suspected that the clear liquid was mostly water, but Charley paid a steep price. She quickly emptied the glass and asked for another. The plump woman had an oval face packed with makeup. She made Charley for the mark and directed her smile toward him. "I'm available now if you would like to escort me upstairs."

Charley was about to say yes when a butler announced the entrance of a Belgian prince, or so he claimed. Dressed in a scarlet uniform filled with medals and fringed with gold braid, he asked for the most expensive courtesan in the house.

"What's a courtesan?" Charley asked Jesse.

"I don't know for sure, but it must be some kind of whore. That's all they got here."

"Young man," Charley's new girlfriend said, "You should make better manners here."

"Ma'am," Jesse replied, "I'll make what you deserve."

With great flourish the butler signaled a grand entrance by Madam Aivoges. Curtains parted, and she walked into the room showing off copper-colored curls piled high on her head. The madam wore a green satin gown with billowing panniers. Her enameled face had several layers of rouge, and a silk scarf covered most of her neck, but Jesse saw aged skin where it gapped. Diamond rings, or most likely good fakes, also drew eyes away from other physical imperfections. The madam walked up to the alleged Belgian prince and curtsied. He bowed and kissed her hand in European fashion. Patrons seemed in awe of their manners.

Jesse spoke quietly to Charley. "It's all a blind. They're trying to give this joint a posh look it doesn't deserve. Let's get out of here." This recognition came courtesy of the Colonel, who had taught Jesse how to quickly see through a curtain of deceit.

Charley's whore bristled, aware that Jesse was cutting into her evening's profits. "Why don't you leave if you don't like the company here. I'll give your friend a night he'll never forget."

"Well, I'm leaving, Charley, are you coming or not?"

Charley hesitated after turning toward the whore. "I got to go with him. My boss told me not to leave his side. Maybe I can see you some other time."

The irritated woman frowned and stomped off.

They next stopped at a barrel house, a long narrow room with rows of beer barrels on one side and a long table on the other filled with empty tumblers. For five cents, customers could fill a small mug from the spigot of any barrel. But if they failed to order additional drinks, several big bouncers threw them out. These large, muscular men beat kickers with slug shots—a short piece of heavy rope with a loop at one end and a chunk of lead tied to the other. Jesse and Charley quickly finished their mugs and ordered bar drinks at much higher prices. Their pick, called Cousin Kelly's Top Drawer Irish whiskey, consisted of one-half water and one-half creosote. Holding their almost full mugs, they walked into an adjacent dance hall without challenge. Jesse attributed this to his companion's size and that the bouncers thought the pair would pay for a dance. That room had unfinished plank walls and a matching floor. Several drunk boatmen staggered around holding loud, sweaty women. A pimp named One-Legged Duffy hobbled about between songs collecting five cents from drunk patrons. The orchestra consisted of an old bald man with a large beard playing a poorly tuned piano, a drunk fiddler, and a young boy trying to master a trombone and failing with every note. The most interesting attraction in the room, however, was a black bear sitting on its haunches in a corner. A large chain held it to a stanchion imbedded in the wall. A sign around the bear announced that "This drunk bear don't dance."

While Jesse pondered the significance of this message, Charley interrupted his concentration. "Them musickers ain't much good."

The boy agreed. "I can't stand this. I'm going back to the boat."

"I think I'll stick it out awhile if you go straight back. May buy me a dance. That gal over there don't look too bad."

Jesse stared at Charley's choice and saw a fat woman with wrinkled hair the color of sauerkraut. He started to offer Charley an opinion about her but decided not to. "Be careful. This place is exactly what the Colonel called it, a hell hole."

After Jesse returned to the steamboat he knocked on the Colonel's stateroom door and received word to enter. The Colonel smiled at the boy's expression. "Well, I see that entertainment Under the Hill did not appeal to you."

Jesse sat down in a chair. "The whole place is sickening. I couldn't stay another minute."

The Colonel closed his book of Byron's poems, and the boy sensed a lecture coming. "You feel that way because you are acquiring the good taste of a gentleman and are repulsed by the wickedness you observed. Keep in mind that there will always be a place for people who choose that life. Dogs always return to their vomit. But do not become an insufferable moralist. You have chosen the wrong profession for that luxury."

Jesse walked onto the hurricane deck to watch the flickering lights of Natchez and considered his recent experiences and the Colonel's assessment. By then he recognized that the Colonel was preparing him for something more than a sporting man's life, but the boy could not discern what it was to be. During this melancholy mood he recognized that his past seemed so far away. Though he did not regret what he left behind, Jesse felt a warm breeze whistling a somber tune in his ears.

4

After two days in Natchez the crew and passengers heard that rumors of Yellow Fever had been false, so *Eclipse* got underway, but without the Colonel and Jesse. When the boy asked why, his mentor explained the decision. "One cannot depend on news from river towns about the existence of Bronze John," the Colonel's name for the fever. "Businessmen do not want to lose profits generated by steamboat landings so they hardly ever admit that fever exists. It may or may not be true in this case, but one should never take the chance. Such men would rather infect everyone aboard than lose a farthing of trade." Jesse would learn that the yellow fever was borne by mosquitoes and periodically killed thousands of people in the Mississippi Valley. The insects flourished in temperatures ranging from 70 to 90 degrees. They preferred to lay their eggs in still water and feed on blood. After contamination, victims become sick in three to six days with fevers in excess of 100 degrees. They suffer from nausea, intense headaches, delirium, vomiting blood, and yellow skin. The fever initially came from Africa to the Americas on slave ships, a fitting irony the Colonel once observed. It acquired the name yellow fever because of yellow quarantine flags used to warn of its presence.

So they boarded *Peerless* and headed north. When the steamer docked at Memphis to load sacks of cotton seed, Jesse and the Colonel walked onto a wharfboat filled with punters. That night several Chickasaw men onboard fancied themselves astute poker players. After declining several times to join the game, the Colonel seemed to reluctantly accept their offer. As play progressed, three young men continued to smoke pipes and drink whiskey, a refreshment that ill-suited any gambler's judgement. Soon one of them began to cheat. He had an old top hat on the table in front of him, and inside the hat a mirror. He could see on his deal every card dealt. After several losses the Colonel spoke up. "Young man, in no way do I intend this to impugn your integrity, but one should never place foreign objects on a poker table. They distract from one's concentration."

The Indians looked at each in search of what to do. The Colonel's words and demeanor were so reasonable, measured, and soothing that they could not take offense. Jesse had observed this technique on many occasions when the Colonel sought to disrupt an activity that reduced his edge. It invariably worked, and in this instance the cheater placed his hat on the floor. None of them detected the Colonel's plan to stitch them up. He held down his winnings until a large blind built up. At that point the Colonel raised big before a draw. All the Indians, including an old chief, called and took three cards each. The Colonel took one and won. The young players quit, leaving the Colonel and chief. He had a man stand behind the Colonel and identify cards using tribal signs. The Colonel did not object and waited for an opening. When it came, he dealt himself two eights and three other cards. The chief took four sixes and a king. Both men placed heavy bets. The chief knew what the Colonel held so he remained confident. At this point Jesse walked up and dropped his drink on the floor. The chief and his spotter turned to look, and the Colonel slipped himself two more eights and an ace, which he rested face down on the table. The Colonel bet heavy while smiling at the chief. This smirk irritated the old man, and he pulled out a pouch with silver coins and put it on the table. The Colonel called and showed his cards. The chief stared and leaned closer to the table, hoping to see things differently. When this did not happen, he looked up at his spotter, pulled out a large knife from its sheaf, and a race began. The younger man made it to the hatchway first, which saved his scalp. Jesse walked out on the main deck with the Colonel and watched the young Chickasaw climb a levee toward Beale Street with the chief in hot pursuit. After Jesse's mentor studied the situation he observed, "I'll bet you ten dollars the chief never catches that boy."

"That's a sucker's bet."

"Most are."

The Colonel departed, but Jesse remained on a promenade admiring lights shining over the levee. It looked like a shimmering sun hovering above the horizon before setting for the night. Strange music and raucous laughter reminded Jesse of his first visit to Beale Street. The Colonel had allowed Schoolboy, an occasional capper, to give Jesse a tour of what the Colonel called a place inhabited by rather peculiar people.

During that tour with Schoolboy, Jesse walked by downtown brothels located in narrow, clapboard houses, some painted, some not. Each held only a handful of whores, but there were plenty of handfuls to go around. Gayoso and Second streets, only three blocks east of the river, provided roustabouts an easy walk from piers to pleasure. Beale Street downtown had become a center for a variety of vices. Nicely turned out slickers displayed gentlemanly manners while promenading down the street. Gaming parlors, bars, and whorehouses lured men wicked and unwise. Customers included white and black men.

Jesse saw all sorts, but stopped in his tracks when he saw Lord Elgin near the Gayoso Hotel. The tall, black man sported greased down straight black hair parted in the middle. He twirled a silver-tipped cane as he walked. A pearl stickpin held down a silver tie over a white shirt. He finished this ensemble with a pinstripe suit and white gloves.

"Who is that?" Jesse asked Schoolboy.

"That's Lord Elgin."

"What is he lord of?"

"The best shebang on Beale. It even sports some white whores."

Beale Street had its dandies, but dangerous men as well, even boys. Schoolboy warned Jesse about them. "Never go down an ally here. Some orphans called the Hot Dozen use bricks for weapons. Boys in Noah's Ark are real good knife fighters. You don't ever want to be here on Monday mornings. The coppers come through and arrest men who still have some money." The courts handed out fines---two dollars for being drunk in public, ten dollars for fighting in the street and twenty for biting off an opponent's ear. Almost anyone on Beale could be arrested for a crime at one time or another, but police only brought in those who had cash or valuables. Judges promoted law and order in the city by splitting fines with arresting officers. Two blocks, one between Beale and Gayoso, the other between Hernando and De Soto, on Saturday nights offered a street show of debauchery with unusual music booming out of juke joints.

The area had loud whores, violent pimps hiding straight razors in their sleeves, and punters, plenty of them. Some women wearing few clothes danced the hoochy-koochy on front porches. Sharpers filled gambling parlors. House players, crooked as grape vines, took substantial rake-offs. From second story windows, pimps watched their whores perched provocatively on front steps. Called sweet men and easy riders, they wore fine suits and expensive jewelry. Pimps played pretty with their girls until too little money made it upstairs. Then they beat them and sent the soiled doves back to their perches.

Jesse first tried cocaine on a Saturday night there. It was cheap and legal in Memphis. Called sniffs, users bought it at drugstores and groceries. Jesse walked into a grocery that night looking for a pint of buttermilk and walked out with a nickel pack of cocaine. This decision came about after he heard another shopper describing its effects. Though enjoyable, it happened only once. When the Colonel found out he threatened Schoolboy. "If this ever happens again I will have you thrown overboard with large rocks in your pockets." Schoolboy was not real smart, he failed the second grade twice, but he recognized the Colonel's seriousness.

The morning after watching the two Indians race over a levee the Colonel expressed some remorse about this affair after Jesse brought it up. "I cannot help but have some sympathy for Indians travelling on rivers. It brings to mind the *Monmouth* disaster." The Colonel paused. "Have I told you that story?"

"No."

"Authorities chartered *Monmouth* to transport Indians west, away from their homeland. It departed New Orleans for the Arkansas River carrying 700 Creeks forced to relocate. One night it collided with *Tremont* being towed downriver by *Warren*. *Monmouth* sank immediately, throwing men, women, and children into the rapid current. More than half of the Indians perished."

"Why didn't the pilots spot each other?"

"It was a dark night, and in their hurry to deliver the Indians and increase their profits, *Monmouth*'s officers entered a passage in the river reserved for vessels heading south." The Colonel finished his story with one of the most emotional declarations that the boy had ever heard. "Damn those black-hearted villains for exposing innocent people to such peril and destruction." The Colonel reflected for a moment, then abruptly changed the subject. "Your statistical calculations are acceptable, and I take it you have finished with Dickens and that volume of Wordsworth's poetry. I think it is time for American authors. We will begin with Fennimore Cooper. He has some rousing adventure stories that you may enjoy."

Jesse greatly admired the Colonel's knowledge of literature and about most other things as well. His judgment appeared to be unquestionable, but the boy eventually discovered a weakness---horseracing. During one stop in Memphis they remained to bet on races at an Olympic Park track. But too many owners doped their ponies, and he could not gain an edge. Soon the Colonel decided to wager at a rural setting in Tunica County, Mississippi, not far from Memphis. A farmer operated a track there. Since nobody in nearby towns owned anything resembling a racehorse when he built it, the owner originally set out to race mules. He soon found out why sporting men never bet on mules. When a pistol shot started a race the mules wandered off in different directions, and no one could do anything about it.

Plus, Crazy Nathan lived nearby. He heard that John Murrell, a notorious river pirate, buried money where the farmer located his track. This caused Crazy Nathan to roam around at night digging holes in search of plunder. Each hole proved to be empty, and they had to be filled before races. Finally, the owner lost patience and put a guard there at night. But the guard being black, and Nathan being white and crazy, this arrangement soon went haywire. After two nights of interruptions by the guard, on his third appearance Nathan wore a white sheet over his head. The guard departed in haste, never to be heard from again. Following a contribution to the county sheriff's widows and orphans fund, deputies convinced Nathan to dig for treasure elsewhere. The Colonel's race betting there ended when two slickers bought the track. He never joined a game with other sporting men so when they acquired the track, he and Jesse caught a steamer in Memphis and departed.

"I heard that Big Oliver and King Langston paid a pretty price for the track," Jesse told the Colonel.

This did not surprise his mentor. The Colonel knew them well and said that they would bet on anything anytime. Both were friends with Freddy Frederick, who also bet on horses. The Colonel said that when Freddy died in Nashville, Oliver and Langston attended the funeral. They sat by the graveside drinking sour mash from a gallon jug while watching two men throw dirt on the coffin. After studying the situation and calculating the odds, Oliver offered to bet Langston on how many shovels of dirt it would take to fill the hole. The drunken Langston went to the grave, looked in it to see how much space remained, and fell in, breaking his nose on the wood coffin. The diggers pulled him out and helped the two finish off their whiskey. Unlike Freddy's coffin, the bet remained uncovered.

After months of internship, Jesse's first solo play began onboard *War Eagle*. He pretended to be a South Carolina planter's son and spotted his mark in the bar. Jesse sat down beside him and complained about losing money in a card game. In telling his story the boy left an impression that he still had a heavy roll and wanted to win back some of his money. Schoolboy came in and talked Jesse into a $100 bet and picked the high card after a shuffle, cut, and spread. This interested the gentleman, who asked to place a bet. Jesse told him that he would not bet less than $100, and the punter agreed. Jesse let the mark win, then left the table to get a glass of water at the bar. Schoolboy marked a winner while the gentleman watched. Jesse returned, and after a shuffle, cut, and spread he asked the mark to pick one. At that point Schoolboy bet $1,000, and the planter followed suit, but he lost. The agitated mark handed over his money as well as a gold ring he pledged for $200. At that point the captain walked in, a good Christian man he was, and spoke harshly to Jesse.

"Have you been gambling on my boat?"

"I could not since it is forbidden," Jesse replied smartly.

"That wouldn't matter to a rascal like you. I don't know how much you cheated this gentleman out of, but you give it back or I'll call the first mate."

"Call who you want, but I will not give up a penny because I earned my money in honest labor before I came aboard. That is sure as gravity."

At this point the nervous loser interceded, saying that they had not been gambling, but playing for amusement. His demurral stemmed from the fact that his wife had given him the ring for an anniversary present. She was in their stateroom and would skin him alive if she heard that he lost it gambling. So the gentleman did not want to kick about the game, fearing that she would find out. He planned to have a New Orleans jeweler duplicate the ring.

However, the captain smelled two rats and dumped one at Hog's Point landing in Arkansas. Jesse sat on a stump in the unusually bright moonlight and took in the scenery. Two green islands ran along the shore with rushes and cottonwood trees. Beyond the landing on each side of a muddy road large trees hosted a chorus of night birds. Their soothing song, along with a Colt pistol, helped him doze fitfully until daylight. The next morning Jesse realized that the landing had been carved out of matted vegetation and willows in full foliage. Sand and pebbles covered the shore. Beyond the clearing a dismal swamp swallowed everything but cypress trees and stumps

Schoolboy told the Colonel about this development, and they stepped off the boat at Natchez and caught *Princess* headed upriver.

The Colonel paid the captain to ensure that his pilot docked at the landing. As the steamer cut hard to port in order to bring the vessel to the bank, Jesse saw the Colonel standing on the main deck, and he appeared to be unhappy.

They walked in silence to the Colonel's cabin. When they entered the boy expected a tongue lashing, but the Colonel reacted in his usual measured manner. "What was your error in this matter?"

"I don't know."

"How much money did you give the bartender for a lookout? You knew about the captain's unfortunate views on gaming."

"I didn't think about that."

"You must always control the odds. You ignored that law to save money and look where it took you."

"Yes, sir," Jesse said, and slept on it.

Unfortunately, the boy's next error in judgment occurred the following night. He was dealing a shaved deck to clip a mark, but Jesse became increasingly concerned about the loser's well-being. His pale complexion and sunken cheeks led the boy to wonder if he had health problems. As his mark's roll grew thinner, the man became listless and spoke in such a pained voice that Jesse strained to understand him. Finally, the punter's head dropped onto his chest. "Would you help me to my cabin? I might not make it without some help," he asked Jesse.

The man attempted to stand and almost fell, so Jesse propped him up and escorted the man to his room. After they arrived, the boy asked, "Will you be alright? I need to leave."

"No. I have not long to live. I have the cancer in my bowels, and it pains me beyond bearing. I'm on my way to Memphis to see my daughter. She will tend to me for my final days. I can borrow enough money to buy a pain easer. Otherwise, I cannot bear it." The man slumped and sighed.

Jesse's better angel whispered in one ear and his worst angel in the other, and the good angel won. The boy handed him $800 the mark lost and departed. Jesse knocked and walked into the Colonel's cabin. His mentor was reading *Marcus Aurelius*, but he looked up.

"I just saw one of the saddest things ever."

The Colonel put down his book. "Tell me."

"I was stitching up this old man in the barbershop and put a hole in his bucket. But I had to help him get back to his room. He is dying, and I felt so bad that I gave him back what I won so he can buy medicine for the pain."

The Colonel smiled. "Was he tall, pale, exceptionally thin, with sunken cheeks, and tufts of white hair?"

"Yes, sir," Jesse answered warily.

"His name is Samuelson, and he has been knocking on death's door for the last 20 years. He is a small time grifter

54

and probably did not make you for a sporting man due to your age until he got in too deep."

The Colonel seemed amused, and Jesse fumed. "This really gets my goat. I've a good mind to go find him and get my money back."

"It is not your money anymore. You gave it to him. I might add that your impulse was noble, but your judgment flawed."

Irritated about his naivete, Jesse asked, "Have you ever given any money back to a sucker?"

"Well, on one occasion I did, but in a roundabout way. I stitched up a young gentleman on *John Simonds* bound for Baton Rouge. After I emptied his purse, he asked me to remain in the bar. When he returned the young man was holding a small velvet box with his wife's wedding ring. I objected to the wager, but he insisted on attempting to pick the lady. I loaned him $1,500 secured by the ring, and he soon lost both. Since it was 3 a.m. I retired, overslept, and had to take breakfast in the ladies cabin with passengers who missed the formal service. When I walked in, there he was, the gentleman I wound up, along with his beautiful wife and wee daughter at the table where a steward seated me. The lady's eyes were red, suggesting great distress. Her husband avoided looking at me after we exchanged a curt greeting. I ate quickly, returned to my room, fetched the ring, and returned as they were finishing their meal. I handed her the ring and told them that a chambermaid found it and asked if I would return the ring to its owner. The husband nodded his appreciation, and his wife clutched the little box as tears fell down her lovely face. How I knew its owner was not broached since we all accepted the pretense." The Colonel paused. "Regardless, I felt better for it, even though a punter benefited."

While in a bar one evening with the Colonel, Jesse observed a well-dressed man come in and order whiskey neat. The tall fellow had a dark complexion, lean body, and a hard look, a really hard look. Still, Jesse eyed him carefully and looked at the Colonel. "He might carry a heavy roll. I'll stitch him up." Jesse expected support but saw that his mentor's equilibrium had wavered.

"Do not approach him...ever."

"Why?"

"I have seen him during other trips. One night when my steamer docked at Vicksburg he came aboard. When he entered the saloon a Mississippi planter walked up to him and expressed his appreciation for something he had done in Mississippi. That man gave the planter the coldest look that I have ever seen. There is something sinister about him, a propensity for cruelty, I suspect. Notice that not one sporting man in the room will approach him."

"Who is he?"

"I know little about him. Word has it that he rode with General Forrest during the war."

"Who is General Forrest?"

"He is a legendary Confederate calvary commander who prior to the war sold slaves in Memphis. Many authorities on military tactics consider him one of the finest cavalry commanders in United States history. After the war he became notorious for leading the Ku Klux Klan, those ignorant villains that you have heard about. I was told by a boat captain that his name is Phillipe Castenau, a former planter from northern Louisiana, and that he sorts out problems that reputable planters need resolved. I am not surprised that he came aboard at Hopewell. The Memphis *Commercial Appeal* has run several stories about a cotton picker union in Lee County. Its members struck for higher wages, and apparently several black strikers were shot by unidentified regulators. Nine others were lynched while on their way to jail in Marianna."

"Do you think that man had anything to do with it?"

The Colonel pondered this question for a few seconds. "I think that Delta planters will never allow challenges to their dominance. I dislike rumors, but there is a longstanding one that men of his ilk are retained to resolve problems, especially those between planters and their workers. I cannot say if the rumor is true, but one thing is. The disputes end with negroes strung up in trees, and I doubt they decided to hang themselves." Jesse heeded the Colonel's advice and avoided the mysterious man.

5

As tutorials continued, Jesse refined his skills, such as cold decking a punter during that man's deal. The boy had extraordinarily large hands, which made this possible. Jesse would hide a deck in the palm of his hand and cut another on the table. A capper would divert attention at critical points to enable the switch. Though they used most of their tradecraft on steamers, occasionally the pair sought marks on trains. Once they left a boat in St. Louis and went to St. Charles by rail. During this train ride the Colonel got skinned, one of the few times in his life. A stranger came in the lounge car and watched the Colonel fumble around in a game of solitaire. The onlooker approached and said flat out that he could pick the right card out of three. He pulled out a roll thick as a flophouse pillow, and the Colonel let him win several $100 bets to set him up. But when the Colonel raised stakes to $1,000 he won, and the mark walked away a loser.

When the Colonel returned to his stateroom with this handsome pot, he learned that the mark had given him a light pack, and only a few outside bills in the roll were real. The others were good counterfeits, but the Colonel recognized them immediately and became apoplectic. "That scoundrel," he said and set out to find the grifter. But the man had wisely jumped off the train. During their search, Jesse wondered how his mentor could declare that man a scoundrel when the Colonel hardly ever played on the square. Perhaps wounded pride, the boy thought, and never brought up the incident.

Jesse only saw the Colonel kick that one time, and his marks rarely complained since the Colonel stitched them up with great skill. However, some less clever slickers did not fare so well. On a memorable occasion, Jesse saw a woman kick like a government mule. When the Colonel suffered from one of his periodic episodes with gout, the boy capped for a sharper named Cotton Joe on *Emma No. 3* heading south out of Memphis. Joe beat a man out of $600, and the loser returned to his room and told his rather large, ill-tempered wife about this questionable loss. She came to the bar carrying a thumbuster revolver, but Joe had stepped out to relieve himself. The woman yelled, "I want my money back or I'll kill the man who cheated my husband." She waved the pistol around, and patrons froze, not wanting to become the first man to die.

The bartender spoke up. "Lady, the man who won your money fair and square stepped out for a moment."

Jesse remained at the table, satisfied that she had not connected him to Cotton Joe. The woman had blood in her eyes and froth on her lips when Joe returned. She screamed at him. "You cheated my husband. You hand over my money or I'll splatter your brains all over that wall." Joe did not believe her and stood pat. The woman's hand shook so bad that when she pulled the trigger from about four yards away the bullet missed Joe and creased the buttocks of a porcine banker on a barstool. He bellowed like a flogged beast, and the human stampede began. The blast scared Joe so bad that he soiled his drawers and jumped overboard, leaving all his plunder in a stateroom to be packed by a porter and unloaded at the next landing. The first mate managed to disarm the woman, and every sharper on the steamer avoided her husband.

Jesse curtailed his capping after this close call and tended to the Colonel during his convalescence. They boarded the latest version of *Sultana* one afternoon and sat on a port side veranda as the Colonel stared silently into space.

"May I ask what is on your mind?"

The Colonel's reverie subsided, and he turned to the boy. "I was thinking about how the name of this steamboat will forever exist in ignominy. At the end of the Civil War an earlier version of *Sultana* loaded at Vicksburg. The steamer had a capacity of about 375 persons, but more than 2,400 men, mostly Federal soldiers who had been held in abominable southern prisons, boarded the vessel. Near Marion it exploded, killing about 1,700 of them. On one of my trips, I met Arthur Jones who was aboard that doomed *Sultana*. He was on the bow when it happened, which probably saved his life. Mr. Jones said the explosion threw him several feet into the air and others off the vessel and into the river. Steam scalded hundreds. Collapsing decks crushed men to death. Others trapped in the wreckage were burned alive. Mr. Jones admitted that he could still hear the screams and pleas of hundreds of men as the fire roasted them. The poor soul is haunted by that tragedy."

Jesse sought something appropriate to say when the Colonel grew silent. "I wonder sometimes why you study history when it depresses you so."

"I concluded long ago that the profound questions, and even some of the answers, may be found in history, literature, and theology. I gave up on theology since its paths too often lead to absurdities. Voltaire observed that a man who believes absurdities will commit atrocities. So I occupy myself with history and literature. You should do the same."

When the Colonel and Jesse boarded *Eclipse* at Memphis the Colonel allowed his protégé to set up a poker game in the bar. At noon, when the room emptied as patrons departed for meals in the cabin, Jesse attempted to give the bartender six decks of marked cards and $50.

The chunky man, with thick red hair and a matching beard, appraised Jesse with a jeweler's eye. "I think you're a bit of a pup to be running brace games. Best be off with your money."

Jesse smiled. "The Colonel said I could depend on you. Was he wrong?"

"You know the Colonel, do you?"

"Yes, sir, and it is with his permission that I approach you with this arrangement."

The man wavered, but Jesse held out $60 and won him over.

Late that afternoon the boy returned and found the room full of slickers in matching duds stitching up punters. He was astonished that anyone would enter a game with men dressed in that manner. Everyone knew their profession, but marks played them anyhow. Jesse once asked his mentor why this was so and received a one-word response --- pride. They want to beat a sporting man for bragging rights.

That day in the saloon three midwestern merchants drinking beer occupied a table with one empty chair. Jesse approached wearing a poorly fitted suit and an air of ignorance that attracted the men, and they invited him to join a game of draw poker. The three introduced themselves as the Allison brothers, E. R., P. R., and S. R. They were heading from Cairo, Illinois, to New Orleans with bulging purses to purchase sugar and other southern staples for shipment upriver to their store. E. R., the oldest and boldest, asked, "Young man, do you often play poker?"

"Not much. Sometimes at home in Missouri with my friends. My papa sent me south to buy cotton in Baton Rouge. I'm thankful you gentlemen have given me a game to pass the time."

Jesse immediately made them for men who considered themselves fair and square but would empty the pockets of an ignorant youth. He recognized after several deals that they were playing on the square, so the boy did not look for his capper, thus breaking one of his mentor's cardinal rules. Jesse let them get a look at his roll, and after several losses he complained, "My luck is downright awful. Would you mind if I ask for another deck from the bar? Maybe it will change my luck."

"Not at all," replied E. R. "Why don't I buy you a lager to compensate for your unfortunate string of bad luck?"

Jesse thanked him and walked to the bar where the barkeep handed him a marked deck and watered black tea that resembled a dark German beer. With these in hand he returned to the table. "I sure hope this changes my luck. My papa will be real unhappy if I lose all of our money." Jesse ran up the pots on deals he won and held down losses on hands he lost in order to avoid suspicion about a brace game. After the boy won back what he previously lost and then some, S. R. grew surly. The short, wiry brother with narrow eyes and bushy brows was about to kick. Jesse saw it coming and decided to stop before it became ugly.

"I'm tired and need to rest. I can hardly keep my mind on the game. Since I've won a lot I propose to bet a final hand equal to your losses as a gesture of fairness." Jesse said this in a soft tone with a resigned expression that the Colonel taught him, and the brothers agreed. Since their losses had reached almost $1,400, another deal would give them a chance to recoup, or so they thought.

S. R. became apoplectic when his high two pair lost to Jesse's three nines. He threw his hand on the table and kicked. "By golly, I don't know where you learned to play poker, but you're too good at it. It makes a man wonder about you."

Jesse remained calm. "I was just lucky, I guess. Or maybe the Good Lord took pity on me. My daddy is about to lose our farm to the bank. This will help us save our home so mama and my sisters have a place to live. I don't know for sure, but good night." Jesse returned his brace deck to the bartender, who switched it with a clean deck in case the brothers demanded a closer look.

The next morning Jesse returned to the empty bar and handed another $60 to the bartender. "Thanks for your help."

"You're welcome. I appreciate the way you handled the kicker, not letting it get nasty."

"Well, I'm learning from the master."

"You are indeed."

Jesse's master also taught a lesson to an obnoxious young blade. During their *Eclipse* journey, an arrogant mark made rude comments about the bartender, one of the Colonel's favorites. So the Colonel decided to reel him in with a fish story after a deck hand landed a huge catfish. The Colonel walked up to the punter and asked, "Have you seen that enormous ocean pike that a man caught. It is something to see. It is a pole buster."

The man answered no and out of curiosity followed the Colonel down to the boiler deck to view this fish. "Old man, that is a catfish, not a pike," the mark said.

About then Jesse walked by with a notebook supposedly taking notes about this fish. The Colonel addressed him formally. "And who are you, young man?"

"I'm an assistant to the buyer of provisions for this steamboat line. I find fish on the fin for them."

"Do you know varieties of fish? This gentleman does not know a catfish from an ocean pike."

This perceived insult really irritated the sucker. "I tell you what I'll do old man. I'll bet you $500 that is a catfish."

The Colonel hesitated, shifting his feet, but finally agreed. "Well, if you insist. Will this buyer's opinion suffice to settle the matter?"

"Certainly," the man replied.

The Colonel decided to sweeten the pot. "Let us give this buyer our money to hold to make sure we both can cover a loss."

This suggestion that the arrogant blade might not be able cover his wager further irritated him, and he growled. "I tell you what I'll do old man. I'll raise the bet to $1,000, and here is my money." The sucker peeled off notes from a heavy roll and handed them to Jesse.

The Colonel did the same and asked Jesse, "Tell us what fish this is?"

"It is an ocean pike, sir, and a corker. The variety that looks exactly like a catfish. It is rare to see them this far north. They are an ocean fish, but sometimes come upriver from the Gulf. Men who do not often fish in the Gulf cannot successfully identify this variety."

The mark's jaw dropped, and his eyebrows rose. "Are you sure?"

"Yes sir. I have bought many of them. They are almost identical to a catfish, but you can identify them from the length of their gills." This was nonsense, of course, but the sucker did not know it.

The man looked at the gills and shook his head. "Well, I'll be damned. That is something." He approached the deckhand who caught the fish. "What kind of fish do you say this is?"

The Colonel had foreseen this event and paid the fisherman $10 for the necessary answer. "It's an ocean pike, sir." That reply closed the deal.

The Colonel walked away with his winnings, Jesse with his notebook, and an incredulous young man with a big fish story.

The pair sometimes faced risks not associated with fools and kickers. Steamboats rarely survived more than three years before being destroyed one way or another.

Danger lurked in river obstructions such as snags, sawyers, drifts, shoals and other obstacles. Additionally, drunk pilots, sleepy pilots and incompetent pilots led to many disasters. Crews stacked cotton bales up to the steamer's top deck. With sparks flying out of their smokestacks the wonder is that any of them made it longer than two years. Jesse saw firsthand the horrors caused by accidents when during winter they took passage on *Belle Zane*. After departing Cairo southbound the steamer struck a snag about four a.m. and quickly sank to the cabin. Crewmen herded passengers in their nightclothes onto the cabin roof, but a strong current caused the cabin to separate from its deck and float away. Forlorn people hovering in icy water nearly knee deep screamed for help. Others prayed beneath a moon hiding behind a mask of dark clouds. Both the Colonel and Jesse picked up several small children and held them in their arms out of the frigid water. Crewmen tore boards off the pilot house and began paddling ashore with children and women riding precariously on the crude raft. Jesse and the Colonel carried children to safety on the raft and went back for more. The boy experienced intense pain from his freezing legs and feared that he would be pulled underwater by the current and swept away. Once he faltered, fearing that he might not survive.

The Colonel put a hand on Jesse's shoulder and spoke quietly. "Now is the time for a steady hand and stout heart. We must see it through, no matter the cost."

"Yes, sir," Jesse responded and continued, guided by the Colonel's calm determination. The pair and several officers were last to climb aboard the raft and reach shore about a mile from the nearest house. Those who had strength remaining carried those who had none. Many passengers, including children, drowned. The racing current swept away their bodies forever.

After that night the Colonel avoided gaming for several days and withdrew to a quiet place within himself. Jesse observed this respectfully, but one morning he broached a question that had been on his mind. "Colonel, do you think there is a heaven?"

His mentor hesitated before answering. "No. I think it was invented by people who are afraid of the dark."

As Jesse perfected his role being a recently ordained priest, he met a real pastor and became further disillusioned. A kick-up occurred between one of the Colonel's former cappers and the preacher. This traveling evangelist went up and down the river holding tent revivals and damning such vices as drinking, dancing, and gambling. Double Donny had been the Colonel's capper until he went out on his own. While Jesse watched their poker game in a large cabin, Donny reduced the weight of the preacher's collection sack by using a shaved deck. Jesse immediately recognized Donny's error. He was knocking down his umpteenth gin rickey and in too big a hurry to fleece this lost lamb. After losing time and again the sucker upturned the table and yelled. "You are a crook and will not keep my money. Now give it back." Donny refused, and at it they went. They hit, bit, scratched, gouged, and pulled hair until both were bloody and rolling around on the deck trying to get more licks in. Neither would give up, and no telling how long the tumbling would have kept up if the first mate had not separated them. The cabin looked like a struggle took place between a half-dozen ratters and their bait. Jesse observed this and remembered what the Colonel taught him. Never try to fast play a mark unless he is too drunk to notice.

The Colonel also had a kicker problem after he and Jesse boarded *B. L. Hodge* out of Baton Rouge. The Colonel skinned some Texas boys, and they wanted to fight about it. The three Texans had been walking around the bar watching poker games when the Colonel opened up a monte table. The cowboys soon sampled the game and won consistently. Jesse wandered in wearing his cowboy duds and watched a few hands. "I'd like to play if you boys let me in," Jesse said, and the boys let him in. Jesse asked the Colonel to show him how the game worked. This his mentor did, and Jesse asked to bet $50.

"You keep your money cowboy. I do not play for low stakes." This appeared to anger Jesse, and he put down $500. Jesse won, and while the Colonel pulled out more cash from a bag under the table Jesse creased a winner. When the Colonel looked up his protégé pulled out $1,000 and bet that he could pick the right card again. The Colonel covered the bet, which caused the Texans to empty their pockets to back Jesse's play. The Colonel shifted the three cards in quick fashion and asked a Texan to try his luck, since Jesse had almost cleaned him out. This eliminated potential suspicions that the new player might be in cahoots with the Colonel. Unfortunately for the Texans, all three cards on the table were marked, and the winner rested in the Colonel's palm. The cowboy studied the three cards and looked at his friends for guidance. None came, and they all grimaced and groaned when their friend picked a loser. Since the Texans bristled at this development, the Colonel opened his coat to show the Colt 45 tucked into his belt. One cowboy still grumbled so the Colonel turned to Jesse. "Do you have a complaint about this draw?" When the Texans looked at Jesse the Colonel replaced a loser with the winner.

"I mean no disrespect," Jesse answered, addressing the Colonel, "but I believe it its best for all concerned if you turn over those other two cards. That would eliminate any doubt about this game being on the square."

"Very well." The Colonel flipped over both cards and showed the winner.

"Thank you, sir. That is proof positive of no shenanigans," Jesse said.

The hornswoggled Texas boys glared, but moved on, sidled up to their friends to borrow money and tried to fathom this mysterious event.

6

Perhaps Jesse's worst miscalculation occurred after the steamer *General Quitman* pulled away from a New Orleans dock. Observing boarders from its hurricane deck to spot potential marks, Jesse saw a short, scruffy man in soiled work clothes supervising the loading of four long wood boxes with side slats. They appeared to be heavy, which intrigued Jesse. He approached the man when he saw him in the saloon. "May I share this table with you?" Jesse asked.

"Sure."

After buying beer for both of them and making small talk, Jesse asked casually, "I saw you supervising freight. Are you a businessman?"

"You might say that. I'm headed to St. Louis with my four alligators. I'm known far and wide as Gator Man."

"Alligators!" Jesse exclaimed with a frown, "What are you going to do with alligators in St. Louis?"

"I know a circus showman up there who is paying me a thousand dollars apiece for them gators. He wants to use them in a show. He is meeting me at the pier with a wagon and the money."

The $4,000 immediately caught Jesse's attention, and he decided to press ahead. By that time several sharpers had opened games in the bar, and Jesse directed the man's attention to their tables. "You may already know this, but never enter a game with those men. You'll come out with your wings clipped every time. But I do enjoy a square game for entertainment on trips such as this. It helps pass the time."

"Me, too," the man said.

Jesse decided to win Gator Man's $4,000 one way or another. "If you want I can get a deck from the barman, and we can pass some time."

"I ain't been on one of these fancy boats before, but the boys back home call me a fair hand with a deck of cards. But I ain't got much money on me."

Jesse walked to the bar for a shaved deck and soon learned that Gator Man had only $600. After he lost it in several deals of draw poker, the punter sank down in his chair and shook his head. "Boy I got troubles now. I needed that money to pay my freight. I don't know what will happen when the freight collector finds out I can't pay them."

Stringer Perdue, who occasionally capped for the Colonel, had been sitting at the bar assessing prospects when Jesse caught his eye. Perdue approached them. "You gents mind if I join your game?"

"No," Jesse replied, "but this game is over."

An old hand at capping, Perdue took the cue. "What I like to do is pick the lady. I've made me a lot of money with her. I'm about the best there is."

The broke mark perked up when Perdue mentioned winning and began to follow their conversation about playing for the lady.

"I lay down the lady," Jesse mentioned, "but only for large stakes."

"Just how large is large?" Perdue asked.

Jesse hesitated, appearing to ponder the question. "I guess $1,000 is large enough."

Perdue nodded and pulled out $1,000. "I'm game. Let's have a go."

Jesse rifled through the cards sloppily for show, found the queen, and placed her and two other cards face down on the table. After Jesse shifted them about, Perdue picked the queen and pocketed $1,000. The capper grinned large and bragged. "Yes sir. I told you so. I can pick her every time. Tell you what. Let's double down and go again."

"Well, you're good, real good. I can see why you win all the time." He hesitated for a moment. "Let me get another pint, and we'll go again. Jesse left the queen and two other cards on the table and walked to the bar with his empty stein.

Perdue bent the queen slightly and smiled at gator man. "That boy don't need that much money no how. Let's lighten his load a tad." When Jesse returned, Perdue pulled out $2,000 and stacked it neatly on the table. "Let's have another go."

But before Jesse could begin his card shifting Gator Man interrupted. "I want in on this."

Jesse turned to him. "Only if you're sure. And you will have to put your $2,000 on the table before the deal."

Gator Man shrugged. "I have nothing now, but I'll have money when I hand over my gators to the circus man. Besides, I might win and not owe you nothing."

"Sir, I'm sorry, but the rules must be observed. You will have to wager cash or post property to secure any losses."

"I got nothing but my gators, and they're worth twice that much."

"Well, they may be if the buyer shows up. But if he crawfishes they are worth very little. Showmen are notoriously unreliable. That is an additional risk I take should I win."

Perdue pushed the negotiation along. "Let's get this done so I can pocket my $2,000."

Jesse nodded and picked up the three cards, but Gator Man interrupted. "All right then. I'll put up my gators. I want in."

Jesse nodded. "To show this is on the square I think you should do the picking," he told Gator Man, "assuming that this gent accepts."

Of course, Perdue accepted. While Jesse manipulated the three cards until the queen rested in his palm, Perdue occupied Gator Man's attention with pleas to quickly find the lady so they could gather their winnings. After Jesse's laydown, all three cards had identical creases, and Gator Man looked nervous, but Jesse insisted that he make the turn. And that is how Jesse came to own four alligators.

It is also how Jesse learned that alligators are inquisitive creatures that can climb stairs, though laboriously. They had been housed in a small enclosure on the main deck set aside for animals, specifically the chef's laying hens and passengers' beloved dogs and cats. The giant reptiles had chomped through the slats and dined on the other animals that shared the space. All that remained were feathers on the deck and a few pet collars. The *alligator mississipiensis*, or so the Colonel called them, climbed the stairs and reached the boiler deck about the time Jesse arrived to examine his winnings. He faced the full force of exceedingly well dressed, hollering, screaming, terrified people running for their lives along the boiler deck and heading for the texas.

Several things helped save the day. The first mate and his crew were mostly Cajuns from Louisiana's rural parishes and had for many years shared the swamps with alligators. The creatures made a tasty gumbo. These men knew that a gator's jaws biting down were enormously strong, but relatively weak when the reptiles attempted to raise them. The first mate rushed his men to the boiler deck stairway, helped passengers move quickly up the steps, and blocked access with large tables turned on their sides. They then brought up long, thick poles used to help push the steamer off a sandbar if stuck. The mates rigged nooses with heavy rope tied to the ends of their poles. Jesse stood on the stairs and watched the amazing sight of these men harnessing his alligators. They pulled the beasts to a deck guard gate and forced them into the river. Down sank Jesse's hopes of a

$4,000 payday as well as his spirits when he anticipated the Colonel's reaction.

It was not long in coming. The Colonel found Jesse in the boy's cabin and chose to stand while upbraiding his apprentice. "You apparently have shown an appalling lack of good judgment. Let me tell you what I have learned from the ship's officers, and you tell me where they are in error. They found the man who boarded with the creatures, but he claimed that he no longer owned them. That you do after winning them. The alligators clearly terrorized the passengers, many of whom insist on exiting the vessel at Port Arthur. Naturally, their ticket costs will have to be refunded. I was told that alligators ate their precious pets. Many children are grief stricken. Tell me what of that is untrue."

Jesse could not make eye contact so he stared at the bulkhead. "I don't know about the pets being eaten, but the rest is true."

"What inebriate thought made you wager on alligators. That is the part that most confounds me."

The Colonel paused, and Jesse glanced at him, but turned away when he saw his flushed face. "I made a mistake."

The Colonel looked hard for a moment or two before continuing. "Here is how the matter has been resolved. I emphasized to Captain Rodgers that you did not crate the animals, bring them aboard, or agree to have them poorly stowed. Those errors belong to an idiot named Gator Man and the ship's deck crew. And by the way, why you would set up a game with someone named Gator Man is another mystery. Regardless, the mates should have been more diligent and rejected that freight at the gangway. However, this gains but a little. The losses and passenger heartbreak are incalculable. I have had to make a substantial payment to the captain to release you from liability, and we are to disembark at the next landing and never again board this vessel. The captain has agreed to put the entire blame on Gator Man so as not to destroy your reputation lest you be called Gator Boy for the balance of your career, which would be brief given that appellation. In the near future you will forfeit all of your earnings to me until I am fully compensated. Let us speak of it no more," the Colonel said calmly after a pause. "The thought of it elevates my blood pressure to a dangerous level

Jesse observed another of his mentor's legal theories in action when a kicker brought charges against the Colonel in New Orleans after *Southern Belle* tied up at the end of Canal Street. While they sipped chicory coffee and ate beignets at Café du Monde, two marshals came to their table and presented the Colonel with a warrant and warned him not to depart New Orleans until his hearing. The Colonel briefly read the forms and expressed outrage. "Certainly, gentlemen. I will not hesitate to appear at the appointed hour and vigorously defend my honor. These are false fulminations of a poor loser." After finishing their drinks the Colonel and Jesse visited an attorney who owed the Colonel money. He provided names of both the judge and prosecuting attorney and that they lunched at Galatoire's on Bourbon Street each day.

The Colonel, dressed like a well-to-do southern gentleman, and Jesse wearing a priest's collar, sat next to the judge and prosecutor after bribing a waiter for an adjacent table. The gentlemen nodded to the Colonel after his greeting, and they began to chat. They also began a bottle of champagne bought by the Colonel, then another bottle. Neither mark appeared to notice that their new acquaintances drank very little. After the judge's nose looked rosy and the prosecutor's eyes got glassy the Colonel invited them to a nearby private gaming parlor. He suggested that Jesse go for a walk in Audubon Park until their game ended. The Colonel explained to the judge and prosecutor that his sister died when Jesse was a young lad, and he became the boy's only surviving heir. "As you might expect, I am the main support this fine young man can count on." After the judge and prosecutor won a substantial sum of money the party broke up with warm sentiments expressed and vows to continue their friendship.

Neither the judge nor prosecutor revealed the slightest recognition when the Colonel and kicker appeared in court two days later. The Colonel explained with gentlemanly candor that he had never seen such bad luck when the loser played him one evening. The kicker called the Colonel a sharper and said that none of his opponents ever walked away a winner, an unfortunate claim under the circumstances. The judge called this a dispute between gentlemen and fined each five dollars for gambling aboard a vessel that prohibited it. The Colonel gave his five dollars to the bailiff, and the kicker stood in front of the bench threatening an appeal, but to no avail.

When Jesse asked the Colonel if he planned another game with the judge and prosecutor to get his money back, his mentor said no. "Never give a dog a bone, then try to take it away."

Late one morning the Colonel and Jesse sat near the fantail and watched a frontiersman practice with his shotgun. Two boys threw empty beer bottles high in the air above the steamer's wake, and the man shattered them before they hit the water. He must have hit about 20 before the boys ran out of bottles and energy. As the man walked away he shoved his gun into a leather sleeve designed for it and nodded to impressed onlookers.

Jesse turned toward the Colonel. "He is a fine shot."

"He is indeed. However, the best marksman I have ever seen was a shootist called Wild Bill Hickock."

"I read a penny dreadful about him. How did you meet him?"

"He was aboard a steamer after touring with Buffalo Bill's Wild West show. He was tall, lean, had tresses spilling down to his shoulders, and a hunter's eyes. Mr. Hickock was an uncommonly good pistol shot. He would stand on a deck guard and bet onlookers that he could kill turtles sunning on floating logs. This with a 45 from a moving steamer, mind you. Naturally, I did not take his wager, but many did to their dismay. I dare say his winnings paid for an extravagant passage. Though he was an avid poker player, none of the sporting men aboard that vessel offered him a game." The Colonel smiled. "Nor did I. It is interesting to note that he died during a poker game in some godforsaken town out West. An irony indeed."

Helena, a busy Arkansas port, contained many desperadoes. Unfortunately, the Colonel and his apprentice landed in that town one fall afternoon when the captain of *Hiawatha* threw them off his steamer for cold decking some punters. The captain, a Baptist deacon, made the Colonel return money won from the steamer's pilot. Captains often dumped sharpers on sandbars in the middle of rivers, which alerted other steamboat captains about their disreputable reputations. Thus warned, officers elected not to pick up these stranded men. In this instance, perhaps the Colonel would have preferred being stranded on a sandbar. He won a big purse from a Helena ruffian who threatened revenge. While the Colonel and several other sharpers enjoyed their meal at a Helena hotel, Jesse roamed the streets looking for a mob of killers.

When he saw a stevedore at the end of a pier, Jesse handed him two bits and asked if he had seen an unruly group of men around the docks.

The man pointed to a nearby pier. "There's a scatteration of them down there."

Jesse found them waiting for the Colonel to arrive and attempt to board a steamer docked there. The boy returned to the hotel, called the Colonel aside, and explained their predicament. "They're waiting for us, Colonel."

His mentor seemed unfazed. "Go to that funeral parlor two blocks down and rent a hearse. We shall make our way to the pier in that. Jesse did this while the other slickers headed back to the landing on foot, and the Colonel gave them time to get there. They saw the mob, but too late. Several had also cheated some of them, and the furious kickers began beating them with thick staves. None of the thugs expected the Colonel to arrive dockside in a hearse, so they paid no attention to it. Only after the Colonel and Jesse brazenly walked onto the main deck did the men attempt to storm *Cora Belle*. The first mate, aware of the Colonel's generosity, had his largest roustabouts block the gangway. Some displayed smiles and large wood clubs with embedded nails. These paddy whackers would receive a bonus if they repelled a boarding party so the mates welcomed a violent confrontation. Several ruffians asked to buy tickets and board the steamer to get revenge, but the first mate refused. "Sorry, but we're full up. Board the next steamer if you want a trip."

After this faceoff the steamer's captain got underway without taking on all the wood he needed for fuel. So he rushed to reach the next woodyard before another vessel overtook him.

When the steamer docked at the Sunnyside plantation landing to refuel, Jesse stood on the boiler deck at dusk and observed a frantic scene. Crewmen and several sturdy deck passengers who helped load wood to reduce the cost of their passage rushed ashore. Illuminated by a large fire, they attacked the ricks of wood like dervish seeking ecstasy. Men shouted, cursed, and rushed as the steamer's whistle pressed them. When the pilot and captain spotted a rival vessel upriver they dashed ashore to push workers harder. "Put your backs into it boys," the captain urged. "There's smoke up the river." The loaders soon finished and climbed aboard. Clanking machinery and a side wheel paddle sent their boat back into the channel. When they docked at Vicksburg, Jesse learned that the vessel would be inspected that morning, and he expressed concern to the Colonel. "What will we do if the steamer is held in port? Do we need to book passage on another boat?"

"I would not worry about that. These supposedly surprise inspections are a brace game. When inspectors come aboard, captains meet them on the quarterdeck to exchange pleasantries and a few tots of good whiskey. Engineers knock grate bars off safety valves, turn back steam gauge hands to honest readings, and give fire pumps a shot of steam to make sure they work. When satisfied, the first mate will rap a capstan three times to signal that the steamer is prepared for its surprise inspection." Sure enough, the steamer passed its surprise inspection.

7

During summers on the Lower Mississippi, steamboats heated up like tea kettles on a hot stove. To counter suffocating heat and wilting humidity Jesse and the Colonel often sat aft on a sternwheeler to catch a bit of breeze generated by its giant paddle slapping the water. Sometimes a bit of spray would refresh them. During one afternoon Jesse observed gusts sweep away the river's rising steam and studied a bayou along the shoreline filled with flowers. "Those are some beautiful flowers," he said to the Colonel.

"They are *nymphea nelumbo*, a splendid specimen. Sometimes its blooms are the size of a hat's crown. They are a version of the New England pond lily."

"Have you traveled in New England?"

"Some when I was about your age, but I prefer southern climes and cultures."

"I don't suppose you will tell me a little about your youth."

"That is correct. I do not suppose I will."

Jesse observed a disastrous creation of nature when a tornado devastated the Natchez port. Thunder rumbled like distant explosions, and the wind screamed before dark gray clouds unleashed an immense funnel. Animals knew what was coming before people did because horses bolted and dogs shivered and cried while people stared nervously at the sky. *Prince* had tied up that morning and prepared for bad weather. The Colonel and Jesse hovered on its main deck beneath an overhang, their backs hugging the bulkhead, where they were protected from wind and rain. This gave them an excellent view of *Hinds,* which had just docked bout 100 yards away. They saw deck hands hurrying to attach extra lines to shore and crewmen stretching a hawser from the pilothouse roof to the forecastle. But preparations were of little help against the swirling menace. It ripped away everything above the main deck and threw pieces and people in every direction. The pair dropped flat on the deck to avoid flying debris. When the funnel finished its work and the wind abated, they stood and assessed the damage. The *Hinds* stern faced upstream with its bow still tied to a pier. Buildings and houses ashore were completely destroyed and wreckage scattered everywhere. Bodies cropped up amid the debris and bobbed in the choppy river. Two steamers floated hull up.

Jesse could scarcely take it all in and turned to the Colonel. "I cannot believe we survived this. How could it come that close and not harm us?"

"Nature's ways are inscrutable. Let us go ashore and attempt to help these unfortunate souls."

The Colonel and Jesse traveled less eventfully on *Thompson Dean* during their next trip. It regularly headed south out of Memphis during Wednesday nights on alternate weeks, usually with several hundred bales of cotton and about 160 passengers. The captain had been a friend of the Colonel for many years and gave Jesse access to the pilot house. He watched the steamer stop at several river towns and landings to add more bales, sacks of cottonseed and people. Jesse studied the east side of the river, which had been developed for cotton growing for many years. On the west side, however, land adjoining the river consisted mostly of swamps filled with cypress and countless interlaced branches of a hoary grey. Rancid brown water remained dead level, two or three feet deep. Numerous cypress knees spread their thick brown fingers above the water like a drowning man seeking help. Below Helena, a few plantation homes had snuggled into snow-white fields of unpicked cotton.

By the time *Thompson Dean* reached Vicksburg it held about 2,000 bales and 10,000 sacks of cotton seed. But with bales stacked 12 tiers high on the guards, Jesse's vision became limited to the powder blue sky stretched over a distant horizon. At Natchez the pilot mentioned a change in scenery. "The cotton plantations are gone. After we get underway you'll have nothing but sugar cane stretching out as far as the eye can see. Steam from sugar mills rises in all directions. In some places plantation mansions are so close to together that they seem to be one village."

On Tuesday afternoons, church steeples in New Orleans rose into view, and at about 4 p.m. the steamer docked at the foot of Canal Street. Jesse saw many black stevedores negotiating to unload cargo. When the Colonel walked onto the pier he said, "I have to pay a visit to my tailor on Canal Street. Do you want to wait here or meet me at the Palace Cafe?"

"I'll wait here," Jesse replied and sat on a cotton bale unloaded on the dock.

As often happened in New Orleans, a man sidled up with a sure thing deal. He opened with a compliment. "Sir, you look like a wise young man with financial resources who would be interested in a capital opportunity."

Jesse smiled. "What is this capital opportunity?"

"I am Captain Roland Parker, recently of *Red Wing*. While docked here I was approached by several gentlemen of means who offered me a sterling proposal."

Jesse quickly recognized the con, even though the man had gone to the trouble of wearing a nice blue uniform embroidered with a gold captain's insignia. His black hair speckled with gray and a craggy face helped him look the part he was playing. But Jesse made him for a four-flusher and decided to wind him up for amusement. "Tell me about this sterling proposal?"

"I know of a first-rate vessel that will be auctioned off to pay creditors. I have inspected the steamer and can vouch for its many good qualities."

Jesse interrupted. "What is its name?"

"That I cannot tell you. I am bound by my word to these gentlemen not to release its identity until after the sale. They fear that other investors might step in since the opportunity is golden."

Jesse nodded as if he accepted the reply. "What do you want from me?"

"I reached an agreement with these investors that I would find an able young man to serve as my executive officer at a handsome salary. There would, of course, be an apprenticeship fee, but the salary would soon offset that charge, and then become bountiful."

Jesse appeared to ponder the proposal for a moment. "How much would the fee be?"

"I think for such prestigious status a charge of $5,000 would be warranted."

Jesse shook his head. "I'm sorry, but I only have $2,000 saved up."

The grifter pondered this development only for a moment. "Well, if I accept your diminished offer could you act immediately?"

"I think so, but I'll have to go to my bank and withdraw the funds."

"Excellent. I'll go with you."

"No. That's out of the question. My father taught me to never disclose my bank to anyone. You'll have to wait here."

"I must confess that I don't see the harm in it," the man said uncomfortably. "Besides, it's dreadfully hot out here."

"I know, but I cannot break my father's rule. He is a bank manager with substantial means, and I will talk to him about investing in the steamer if any shares remain. He's always on the lookout for opportunities like this."

The so-called captain's focus switched from the heat to this new opportunity. "Perhaps you could introduce me to your father when you visit the bank. We might go together with his permission. I assure you that I can make available additional shares for purchase. My investors will be glad to share the opportunity. They are reasonable men."

"We'll see. If you remain here I'll soon be back with the money. But if I see you following me the deal is off."

"I must say that this is highly irregular and not the way I prefer to do business."

"That may be, and if you don't want to follow through I'll understand."

"Very well, but please hurry. This heat might cause a stroke."

Jesse walked down Canal Street toward the tailor shop where the Colonel had his bespoke clothes made. After assuring himself that he had not been followed the boy took a seat in the small reception area and considered with some pleasure that he had easily outplayed an experienced grifter.

The Colonel soon walked out of the fitting room and saw Jesse. "I thought you were waiting at the dock."

"I got bored, but I do have a good story for you. They went to the Palace Café across the street for a glass of iced tea, and Jesse shared the steamboat story. At the end of it he said, "I almost felt sorry for the poor guy. His game is so thin you can see right through it. I don't know how he could ever clip a mark with it."

"I assure you he will find some fool to stitch up. As I have told you more than once, never put money in a steamboat venture. They are invariably a disaster."

"I know. I played him for amusement."

The colonel's expression darkened. "We never play for amusement. We are always serious since the play can be dangerous. Never forget that."

Jesse accepted the criticism and changed the subject. "Why do you have such strong feelings about steamboat investments?"

The Colonel leaned forward to share a story. "One of my best cappers, a man called Big Bill, came to me with a sure thing deal on a vessel. Mind you Bill was an experienced capper who should have known better. He and a man who called himself Captain Young bought *Glasgow* at a marshal's sale. According to Bill, the steamer would go into White River-Memphis trade hauling 1,000 bales of cotton at $2.50 per bale each run, making four trips per month. If the steamer only brought in half that amount on the return trip its total income would be $15,000 per month. Naturally, I knew better and declined Bill's offer to invest in his venture. Unfortunately for Bill, on its first round-trip from Memphis to the White River the vessel's receipts amounted to only $350. Young had no experience piloting a steamboat, so *Glasgow* ran aground and had to be pulled off a sandbar. That cost $200. It lost a smokestack in Black River. By the end of their first trip the partners came up $5,000 short. Keep in mind that their experience is typical, not unusual."

Jesse followed the story and became increasingly amused as the disaster unfolded. "Does anyone ever make money running steamboats?"

"Rarely, except for the large combines, who fix prices at steep rates. Many independent owners must borrow money to buy boats or build them. They pledge their farms, homes, and other possessions to guarantee loans. Most lack sufficient financial resources to operate so they lose everything when lenders foreclose. Risk has led to insurance rates most owners cannot afford. They go broke paying for insurance or go broke not paying for insurance when their vessel disappears in a cloud of smoke and hissing water. It is a sucker's bet. Never forget that."

Jesse saw evidence of this when *J. M. White* burned to the waterline. While heading downriver aboard *Picayune,* passengers and crew could see flames and smoke shooting skyward from a Blue Shore, Louisiana, landing. The *White* had pulled into its pier to load cargo. Built for Captain John Tobin, Jesse heard that the steamer cost a fortune. That night it held more than 3,000 bales of cotton, 8,000 sacks of seed, and 400 barrels of oil. A mate on shore loading cotton saw the fire and raised an alarm. The crew woke passengers and told them to make their way to safety. *Picayune* maneuvered to a respectful distance and sent small boats to rescue people hovering on the stern.

While watching the disaster from *Picayune*'s bow, Jesse turned to the Colonel. "I hope everyone makes it off."

"I do as well, but in these cases some fools attempt to save their trinkets and die trying. It makes one wonder about a connection between greed and idiocy."

Helena remained on the Colonel's list of port towns to avoid, and he declined to go ashore there. He stressed that it displayed many of the vices found in New Orleans, but none of the charm. Jesse knew that the port's wharf master had to contend with a variety of shady characters and criminals. He described some of them when Jesse walked with him on a pier. "Shanty boats hide ruffians and murderers evading the law. Minstrel troupes have women who moonlight behind boat curtains. Some barbers, called tooth jumpers, take out teeth with mallets and metal punches. They give their patients tanglefoot moonshine to dull the pain. When barbers punch out the wrong tooth they start all over again. Sharpers lighten pocketbooks using a lot of grifts." Jesse soon observed one of them. He stepped onto the pier late one afternoon and heard shouting from a large tent in the distance.

Drawn to the noise, Jesse stood shocked by what he saw after joining the crowd. A preacher, or so he claimed, stood at center stage and appeared to heal cripples and cast out demons. A long line of men waited their turn to be dealt with one way or another by this faith healer and exorcist. Jesse moved closer and watched the drama play out. The boy's experiences observing slickers and punters gave Jesse some ideas about the stacked hand being dealt these country folks. Men in the healing line he took to be cappers, pretending to be crippled. Many who claimed to be possessed by demons had been caught by their wives while fornicating with other women. Naturally, they blamed the devil rather than themselves. These men walked up on the stage sheepishly and faced their exorcist. He carried a vial of clear liquid supposedly taken by him from a pure spring after the Lord led him to the water. While deep in prayer at the spring this shyster claimed to have seen an angel bless the water and tell him to dose possessed people until they vomited out the evil spirit. His victims did since the potion's ingredients immediately induced vomiting. During their heaving into a tub the exorcist laid hands on them and shouted. "Jesus saves! Come out you sons of Satan!" The crowd followed suit, screaming, "Jesus saves! Come out you sons of Satan!"

Every time a man threw up in the tub a donation basket made the rounds.

Jesse soon walked away and returned to the steamer. He found the Colonel sipping a glass of Rhine wine in the bar between games and sat down beside him. "You would not believe what I just saw. A grifting evangelist and healer is holding a revival in a field and is shearing the sheep like nothing I have ever seen. We may be in the wrong game."

The Colonel shrugged. "Not even I am sufficiently hypocritical to profit from their fantasy's creations. Though La Rochefoucauld did point out that hypocrisy is a tribute that vice pays to virtue." The Colonel thought for a moment. "The preacher you witnessed brings to mind an incident on *Princess*. The steamer blew up after departing Baton Rouge while I was running a faro table in the barbershop. We heard the warning of hissing steam just before the boilers exploded. The boat's midsection, where the barbershop was located, had numerous sporting men who survived untouched. But 14 preachers, among many innocents, were sent into eternity without a moment's warning. It pushes me closer to deism."

"What is deism?"

"It is a religious concept that you should explore, which reminds me that you also should look into Thomas Aquinas, a brilliant churchman. Meanwhile, we have a boat race to handicap."

A proposed race between *J. B. Galloway* and *Chickasaw* was to begin the next day at Helena and end in Memphis. But the Colonel could not gather enough dependable information about the steamers to be comfortable placing a bet either way. Those on both sides appeared to be banking on assumptions, a word the Colonel called the mother of all mistakes. Won by *Chickasaw*, this race prompted the Colonel to tell Jesse about his only duel. While they lounged in deck chairs the next morning with their coffee the Colonel told the boy his story. "It came about after the famous race between *Robert E. Lee* and *Natchez*. I learned that a man at my gaming table piloted *Lee*. As he drank more and lost more the pilot bragged about winning big in the coming race. I pressed him, and he said that Captain John Cannon planned to strip his vessel of spars, dunnage, passengers and freight and arranged to have coal barges midstream upriver so he could refuel without docking. After hearing this I bet heavily on *Lee* and won big. Those who bet on *Natchez* put up a big kick after hearing of Cannon's maneuvers. They declared it cheating, and many refused to honor their wagers. I bet with four gentlemen, and they avoided me. Even then, I could shoot a pistol with impressive accuracy and demanded to meet the kicker who owed me the most money. We confronted each other on a muggy morning beneath oak trees on a nearby plantation. The kicker's round went high, thank god, but mine hit the man's right shoulder. It dropped him, and I walked up to the gentleman. "You, sir, should know that I could have put that shot through your heart, but chose not to. You owe that debt to your wife and children. You owe your racing debt to me. Now be so kind as to hand it over." His second pulled out a thick roll and settled up. After hearing about the Colonel's skill with a pistol the other kickers made good on their losses. "The news spread about town, and I have never again had a problem with such defaulters."

On a rare occasion Jesse opened a game that the Colonel predicted would be fruitless, but the boy proved him wrong. A capper named Sure Sam approached Jesse while waiting on a train bound from St. Louis to Hannibal, Missouri, scheduled to depart the next day. The train would be filled with couples carrying thick purses on their way to a horserace in that famous river town. Sam needed a stake to finance his wheel game. The plan was to buy jewelry in St. Louis, some valuable, but most not. Sam knew a pawn broker who would sell him a few real jewels and a lot of very good fakes made by a former jeweler who did time in a Carbondale, Illinois, jail for fraud. Sam's problem was that the pawnbroker was too smart to front money for grifters. Since Sam only had $4,000, he needed a partner. Jesse threw in $4,000, and they visited the pawn shop and walked out carrying bags filled with items.

Sam had worked his con on a western stretch of the Missouri River with much success. He set up what resembled a roulette wheel with numbers on it that matched numbers labeled on jewelry items displayed on a table covered with black velvet. Several wheel numbers were blank, so each turn did not show a winner. And Sam had slightly narrowed the numbered grooves that matched expensive pieces and rubbed those spots with olive oil. On fake jewelry stops he applied clear molasses. Though all the stops looked the same, his tricks shifted the odds significantly in the bank's favor. Sam offered the conductor a generous rake off in order to set up the game in a lounge car visited by men and women. "That is the key," Sam told Jesse. "We want all these women seeing what we got and spreading the news all over the train. Women got no sense about brace games. They just fancy what they see and want to spin for it. The good thing about them is they'll keep on trying, over and over, and their gents got to stake them. They hate to say no in front of a bunch of their friends."

Though Jesse expressed some reservations about charging $100 a spin, that perhaps it was too steep, he depended on Sam's experience. Jesse's job was to help spread the news about Sam's wheel and its wonderful prizes. This became short work. After returning to the lounge car following a round of shilling, Jesse found the space packed full of grinning, jabbering women anxious to spin the wheel. As the boy worked his way toward the table of jewelry, he heard women fretting that a particular piece might be won before they had a chance to land on its spot. Jesse watched Sam rake off hundred dollar bills and stuff them into a case on his lap. Women kept trying to hit a number while their husbands or gentlemen friends frowned, grew impatient, but ponied up. When women won something they squealed and became the envy of nearby punters. The spectacle went on for several hours, but some expensive pieces remained on the velvet when Sam closed up shop. He complained of an asthma attack since the room had filled with cigar smoke. Sam promised to give these women another chance during their train ride back to St. Louis, but he had no intention of doing that. It was a short con, not a long one, which greatly reduced a grifter's risk. Their game cost the Colonel a small fortune since only a handful of men had time or money to bet with him.

8

Throughout the months of Jesse's apprenticeship, he sometimes experienced regret about his activities at the gaming tables but saw nothing of it in the Colonel. However, the boy saw a soft spot one afternoon in Baton Rouge. To spot punters they stood casually against a main deck bulkhead observing cabin passengers boarding *Ohio Belle*. A crying woman, thin and haggard, with three young children huddled by her side, walked out of a main deck hatch into the sunlight. The Colonel approached her. "Madam, may I be of assistance?"

The woman stopped sobbing long enough to explain that she could only afford deck passage for them in a space so crowded that they had to stand. "My children have endured nature's noxious odors and human filth for hours at a time, and they are exhausted." The woman said her husband recently died of typhoid fever, and she was returning to Illinois to live with her parents.

"Madam, please remain here until I return," the Colonel replied and nodded to Jesse. They climbed gilded stairs into the plush cabin. There must have been a dozen gaming tables in use, and the Colonel went to each of them and told her story. He collected sizeable donations from sharpers and punters.

They found the chief steward and learned that unfortunately all the staterooms were booked. The Colonel knew Captain Leathers well, and they located him in the pilot house. After learning of the woman's plight, Leathers turned to the pilot. "Raymond, you share a berth with Clyde until this lady arrives safely." Raymond frowned, but went to move his things to another room.

The Colonel thanked Captain Leathers and gave him a hearty handshake. After the Colonel and Jesse found the chief steward and told him which room had become available, they returned to the main deck where the mother and children stood forlornly. When the Colonel told her of this good fortune she swooned, and he supported her. Jesse went to the deck area, found her steamer trunk, and they all paraded up to her spacious room. The chief steward had begun to tidy up when they walked in.

The Colonel took out the money he collected and offered a tip to the steward, who shook his head forcefully. "I cannot take that. Captain Leathers said that all her services are his compliments, and I have advised our staff of this. She will travel first class and pay nothing for the remainder of her passage."

The thankful woman sat on the bed and sobbed. Her children took this to mean more bad news and began to cry as well. But the Colonel sat beside the widow and shushed her. So as not to further upset her children the woman composed herself, kissed the Colonel on the cheek, then smiled at her children. They sensed a change in fortune and settled down. After giving her the donated money, they said goodbye and headed toward the cabin to set up a monte game.

As they walked away, Jesse swelled up with pride. His mentor noticed and warned him. "Keep in mind that he who lives with virtue lives alone."

Jesse nodded his understanding but believed that the Colonel had more on his mind. So the boy spoke out of turn. "May I press you for your thoughts on the matter?"

The Colonel continued to walk. "Let us go to the texas and have lemonade before we set up." After they settled on two deck chairs the Colonel opened up. "The lady we assisted has a shade of hair that reminded me of a long-ago moment. While enjoying a dance in the *Magnolia* cabin one night I met many fine ladies, among them a comely widow. She had auburn hair, a pearl complexion, and carried her ample figure with grace and confidence. Juliet and I waltzed and went to the texas promenade for a quiet stroll before I bid her adieu. I considered this lady the most adorable woman I had ever met, and I joined her the next day for breakfast in the ladies cabin. Before we said goodbye she invited me to visit her Louisiana plantation. I soon accepted and found the manor magnificent. During my sojourn there she set a sumptuous table. After dinner, Juliet played her piano for me with uncommon skill. I avoided telling her my profession, fearing it would lessen her opinion of me." Here the Colonel mused for a moment. "After several days of deception on my part I departed for New Orleans to play the bank at Fitzgerald's."

"Following several days of gaming I arrived one evening at the Monteleone and found a message from Juliet inviting me to meet her for brunch the next day at Antoine's. I declined, sending her a note that I had to leave that afternoon for St. Louis aboard *Vicksburg*. While preparing to board I saw Juliet on the pier and made my way to her. I took the liberty of kissing her on the cheek, and she reciprocated warmly then asked why I seemed determined to avoid her. After an anguishing silence I told Juliet the truth, that I was a sporting man and lived a life unsuitable for a lady of her station. Julia asked if I did not consider her worth a change of profession, and I have never faced such a difficult question. The lady was assuredly worth anything she asked for, but not from me. I had chosen my life's work and declined her offer. Julia handed me a large diamond ring and told me to return it if ever I changed my mind. I demurred, but she walked away. I still have that ring and my gnawing regret."

Jesse soon fell victim to desire for a beautiful girl. After *Kenton* docked in New Orleans, Slim Willie took him on a Storyville tour like no other. A long-time associate of the Colonel, Willie had a gallon of knowledge about the city and poured it out incessantly between swigs of Kentucky bourbon from a tickler flask. At that time city officials confined whores and other unsavory professionals to five blocks on four streets and three on six others. These streets sported wall-to-wall brothels, saloons, and gaming establishments. Some whorehouses looked posh, but others not so much. In one-story crib shacks women lured customers inside with obscene displays of what Willie called kooch. "Why would anyone go in there?" Jesse asked.

"Because it only costs a dollar for whatever a man fancies."

Swanky establishments on North Basin Street usually charged top dollar for intimacy of one sort or another, though additional costs ran up tabs. Customers had to buy expensive drinks before a stable of women were trotted out for inspection. The rooms usually had red velvet furnishings in a Victorian style, and for special rates a gentleman could rent one by the hour with mirrored walls and ceilings. White and black whores could not occupy the same houses, but owners got around that by working them in adjacent ones with connecting passageways. This area came to be named Storyville after the politician who thought a designated vice area was a good idea. He lived to regret it.

To pick and choose from these many attractions, street hawkers sold a tabloid called *Mascot* every Saturday for five cents. Willie bought a copy and turned to the society section. He read several entries to Jesse. "'Madame Julia Dean has received a draft of recruits, and the fair Julia is bragging loudly of her importation. She seems to forget that the ladies played a star engagement here last winter at Haley's, and they all carry their diplomas with them.' This looks like a good one," Willie added. "'Nina Jackson, who keeps the swell mansion, 1559 Customhouse Street, and who is herself one of the jolliest girls in the bunch, has gotten rid of those two tid-bits, May and Mamie, and in their stead she has two of the finest and most charming ladies to be found anywhere. Queen Emmette, known as the Diamond Tooth, is one of the girls, and Etta Ross is the other.'" Willie continued. "Listen to this. 'Josie Alton got thrown out of a house for brawling. Seems she got in a fight on Burgundy Street with Beulah Ripley.' According to this write-up she staggered from the scene of combat minus part of her lower lip and half an ear."

The society section held many lurid entries, and Jesse soon tired of hearing about them. "I've never seen anything quite like this before," he told Willie.

In their ramblings around the French Quarter Jesse saw more than one shop selling voodoo potions. He stepped into a small one to see a black sorcerer named Doctor Beauregard who sold love charms for five dollars. He made them with beef hearts scented by spices and perfumes and wrapped in white crepe. If left at a door the inhabitant could not resist, or so the doctor said. The magic man tied up his long hair in curls that held packets filled with spellbinding items. His curls had pebbles, shells, a dried lizard and frog, a bird skull, and a small hoot owl's head. Though the sight seemed natural for Willie it shocked Jesse. "Why would anyone pay good money for this trash?"

"Don't speak ill of it," Willie replied. "It can work."

"How do you know?"

"I saw for myself one night. I knew a colored boy named Shorty. He was the son of a voodoo queen, and she let him take me to this special house by Lake Pontchartrain. A dozen or so men and women were sittin' on the floor buck nekkid. In the middle they had candles and some other stuff. All sorts of things were goin' on. After a while some women started dancing and twisting around. They got so worked up they fell to the floor and started frothin' at the mouth like a played-out racehorse. I got out of there. I didn't know what was about to happen next, but I didn't want no part of it. I've seen men and women do the dandy right out in the street in front of people after taking a potion."

The voodoo doctor also performed minor surgery. Called a wart taker, he gave patients a secret potion to block out pain while he scraped off and dug out warts with a straight razor. However, sometimes the secret potion didn't work well, and screams could be heard throughout the French Quarter.

As they continued their tour Jesse recognized sharpers in games who also worked aboard steamboats. Though legal gaming had been an off and on thing in the city, according to Willie, laws mattered little. Corrupt cops and justices either ignored violations or benefitted from them. Even when punished, gamblers paid a few dollars in fines before being set loose. Jesse and Willie walked along St. Charles between City Hall and Canal Street and saw about a dozen sporting houses in that stretch. Many had three floors, with faro on the first, roulette on the second and keno on the third. But every floor had small poker rooms. Willie said flat out that none of them were on the square. Jesse walked into Bill Franklin's place on the corner of St. Charles and

Common and observed many skills the Colonel taught him. "Let's get out of here," he told Willie.

Though Jesse did not figure it out until later, Willie steered him to a three-story marble palace on Basin Street. It held Kate Townsend's luxurious brothel. "Let's go in," Willie insisted.

Jesse looked up and down the limestone edifice with thick pillars and asked, "Is this a bank?"

"Might as well be. Come on."

"I don't know. They might not want us in there. Look in that window at those swells. Some are wearing tuxedoes."

"There's some highfalutin' gents in there. That's for sure," Willie said after looking through the window. Both Willie and Jesse were dressed well, but not that well. "Come on," Willie urged, and herded Jesse through the front door. The boy looked around the parlor and saw a fireplace and mantel of white marble and polished black walnut furniture covered in red velvet. Oriental carpets covered the floor, and red paper covered the walls. A sweet aroma filled the air, and demure female laughter danced about the room.

Kate Townsend walked up wearing a low-cut dress showing off the largest breasts that Jesse had ever seen. He didn't know God made them that big. The bordello mistress smiled at his shocked expression. "You must be the Colonel's young associate. Am I right?"

"Yes, ma'am." Jesse felt uncomfortable among these distinguished men in formal evening wear and young women in gowns, and Townsend saw it.

"You are welcome here. And the most handsome man in this room," she said.

After this comment Willie began his exit. "I got to get back. I'll see you later."

"Where are you going?" the boy asked nervously.

"I got to run some errands for the Colonel."

Jesse started to follow him out, but Townsend took his arm and escorted Jesse to the bar. "Normally I would explain the rules, no bawdy talk or disrespectful behavior, but the Colonel vouched for you and assured me that you are a gentleman. Elisa will fit you with a coat and tie." A maid suddenly appeared with each and helped him on with them. "We do have protocols you must observe. You have to buy a bottle of champagne to share with your young lady."

Jesse gulped. "Ma'am, how much does that cost?"

"Our best champagne is $20 a bottle."

Jesse gulped again. "Ma'am, I don't have that much on me. I only have about $15."

Townsend smiled as the boy scrounged through his pockets searching for money. "You don't need cash here. The Colonel has an account, and your expenses will be billed to him."

At this point a hostess led in a pretty young woman about Jesse's age if not younger. She walked up to him and put her hand in his. "I am Loretta, and I am pleased to make your acquaintance," she said softly. Jesse smelled lilac perfume and admired her porcelain skin and luminous green eyes, both set off by long black hair. But he wondered why she was standing so close to him. "I would like a glass of champagne," Loretta said, and a bartender wearing a tuxedo immediately popped a cork and poured. Townsend smiled and excused herself. Loretta stood so close that her body made a tight fit with his. She smiled and looked deep into Jesse's eyes. That is how it all started. It ended the next morning in a plush bedroom with red walls and a mirror on the ceiling. The girl had pleasured him in several ways, and Jesse realized that Loretta knew a lot more about some stuff than he did. After his embarrassed goodbye to Loretta, the boy walked to the Monteleone and up gilded stairs to the Colonel's luxurious suite. After he entered, Jesse blurted out his primary concern. "Colonel, I think I spent a lot of your money last night, but I don't know how much. The girl said she was a virgin, and that cost $20 more."

The Colonel smiled. "You most likely did, but that is my concern." He folded his New Orleans *Picayune* and placed it on a table. "Sit down and let us chat." The Colonel waited until Jesse made himself comfortable before beginning. "Your introduction to things of that nature was coming sooner or later. I wanted it to be of a better sort than what some knucklehead capper would lead you into. Such matters are inevitable for young men. Appreciate the experience, but do not give it more weight than it deserves. Pleasant memories cannot survive much scrutiny"

Jesse pondered his remarks before speaking. "Please don't take this wrong because it's none of my business, but why do you have an account there?"

"The second floor has a gambling parlor reserved for men with substantial wealth, and I occasionally bank games there for a handsome rake off." Jesse had more questions but remained silent. The Colonel told you what he wanted you to know, and that was all.

A potential consequence of his sexual adventure soon sent Jesse into a downward spiral. When he and a bald capper called Curly walked into a saloon, Curly saw a slicker named Tom sitting by himself at the bar. Curly led Jesse over for an introduction and asked Tom, "Is that St. Louis doctor doing you any good?"

"Sometimes. Sometimes not. Sometimes it stinks and hurts so bad I'd cut if off if I didn't need it to piss."

After a minute or two of small talk Curly and Jesse moved on. "What's wrong with him?" the boy asked when out of earshot.

"Tom was a ring-tailed tooter with the women, but he should have kept his pecker in his pants. He got the wapsy from a Vicksburg whore. Some doctor in St. Louis is supposed to cure it, but he ain't done it yet."

Jesse pondered this possible problem in light of his night with the pretty New Orleans whore, and he became exceedingly uneasy. "How long does it take before you know if you got what Tom has?"

"Don't know for sure. Why?"

Though Jesse appeared calm, his gut tightened up when he heard that news. "Nothing in particular. I just wanted to know."

He wanted to know so bad that after supper Jesse asked the Colonel about the wapsy. His mentor described the venereal disease and that the brothel Jesse visited offered only clean girls so the boy had nothing to worry about. But the Colonel closed with this advice. "Do not forget that a wise man walks a narrow path." Jesse nodded and decided to narrow his path in the future.

9

Another opportunity for amusement, but of a different sort, occurred when *Ashland* tied up at a pier next to the Chapman Theatre showboat. When Jesse asked the Colonel to join him for an evening of entertainment his mentor declined. So the boy paid six bits for a ticket and climbed aboard. The show commenced on a stage at the stern with large candles for footlights. It began with a one-act drama about Othello; followed by a monologue from a Greek writer Jesse had never heard of; impersonations of black minstrels; can-can dancers from Paris, and the main attraction, Carlos Donetti's Great Parisian Troup of Acting Monkeys, Dogs, and Goats. The curtain closed after that. When it reopened the stage contained amazing sights -- chirping birds; a stuffed bear and wolves about to fight; a live monkey on a chain; wax figures of the twelve apostles, and large paintings of historic events such as Washington crossing the Delaware. Jesse believed that he got his money's worth. After listening to him describe this extravaganza the Colonel suggested that he should spend less time looking at prancing monkeys and more time studying history.

Since the Colonel was out of sorts due to a migraine, the chief steward had delivered a splendid meal to his stateroom. A braised brisket of lamb with green peas and a desert tray holding several selections. They remained untouched. Jesse eyed the tray and saw a favorite.

"Do you mind if I have the white Windsor pudding with vanilla sauce?"

"Help yourself, but leave the la fleur de orange; that is my choice." The Colonel paused and pondered his situation. "Don't ever grow old and ill. It is irritating." Jesse nodded, quickly finished the pudding, and spoke well of the pastry chef before departing.

The next afternoon Jesse enjoyed another captivating sight, watching roustabouts load cotton onto a vessel while supervised by a steamer's mud clerk. On a cool afternoon during a trip north on *Jefferson* the steamboat pulled into Cigarette landing in Arkansas to pick up dozens of stacked bales. Jesse stood by the gangplank as loaders propelled the 500-pound oblong blocks of compressed lint down a muddy bank onto the loading stage and main deck. They guided bales with cotton hooks to control their speed and direction.

An acrobatic deckhand rode some down to show off. He took great risks. If the bales didn't slide straight, if not guided just right, they might catch on a cable supporting the gangplank. If that happened the man could be crushed and tossed into the murky water. But with great skill he survived to the delight of observing passengers.

Jesse later asked the Colonel how the location became Cigarette landing and learned why. *Swain* was steaming downriver from Memphis when it passed the head of Island No. 40 on its west side. About a quarter of a mile below the island were two wagons loaded with household goods close to a timber opening along the river. A young girl stood beside them hailing the boat. Since the pilot assumed it was a shipment, he cut to starboard and pulled into the landing. The girl ran to the riverbank and hailed the captain, who asked what she wanted. The girl and her brother had been tasked with leading mules hauling items to a new cabin her family had built; she had nothing to ship. The girl only wanted a pack of cigarettes. With a wry grin, Captain Powell sent a porter to take the pack ashore. The girl yelled "thank you" and returned to the woods. And that location became Cigarette landing.

Two weeks later, while aboard *Chas. Bodeman* headed south, Jesse and the Colonel had little to entertain them. The vessel tied up at a Memphis pier because the river had iced over. Most wealthy passengers went ashore for entertainment, so gaming opportunities withered. One morning the Colonel handed Jesse two books to read: U. S. Grant's memoirs and *Uncle Tom's Cabin*. "Why these two?" Jesse asked.

"Because one author helped start the war, and the other helped end it. The match between Grant and Lee has much to teach those of us who live by contest and conquest. You should learn from their different strategies. The study of that history gives us vast stores of incidental knowledge."

Jesse took the books to his cabin, but soon set them aside. He focused instead on the evolution of his relationship with the Colonel. It began as a business arrangement, but after a few months turned into something akin to a father-son bond. At first the Colonel called him a boy, but now addressed him as a young man, which greatly pleased Jesse. Sometimes Jesse felt like an empty clay vessel that the Colonel was molding to store his wisdom and knowledge.

These and other matters brought a thoughtful respite from gaming when ice flows stranded *Bodeman* and dozens of other steamers and strangled traffic on the Lower Mississippi. Even in port, disasters piled up. Jesse watched ice jam together *Nick Longworth* and *Illinois* with great force and reduce them to splinters. Heavy chunks destroyed other vessels as well. Crushing ice pushed *R. P. Walt* into a bank and shattered its hull. Fortunately, *Bodeman*'s captain had commanded several vessels in Upper Mississippi trade and often experienced icy rivers. He avoided crowded piers at the foot of Beale Street and tied up near the mouth of Wolf River. While *Bodeman* rested, Jesse visited its pilot on the bridge and asked Rufus Styles about his training and when he thought he was ready for the job. The answer fascinated Jesse. "This river is about a thousand miles of treachery. My training didn't end until I could shut my eyes and trace it from St. Louis to New Orleans. When I learned to read the face of water like a newspaper. The problem is the river changes something every day. That's where intuition and sometimes good luck come in."

"You need to think about being a sporting man. With your memory and a little risk you could get rich."

Styles grinned. "I say hello to risk every time I climb into a pilothouse and know that the lives of all these people are in my hands. Getting rich I don't care much about. Never have."

Jesse walked away uneasily, recognizing that Styles used his skills to protect people. Jesse directed his talents to harm them. However, he had learned to block out the guilt that at first troubled him, and his doubts disappeared when the cards were dealt. Still, Jesse recognized that the pilot had something to be proud of, and he did not.

The disasters that Styles sought to prevent remained a constant risk on Delta rivers. One that occurred on a warm afternoon during the following spring crushed Jesse's spirits. He and the Colonel heard a distress signal from downriver at about 2:30 p.m. while running a faro game in the *Yazoo* saloon. Gaming tables quickly emptied, and players joined other passengers on the hurricane deck watching smoke drift skyward from a magnificent steamboat. As flames spread aft along a row of cotton bales an onlooker shouted, "That's *Mary Bell*!"

"Are you sure?" Jesse blurted out, shocked by seeing his first love cremated.

Another man agreed with the first. "He's right. That's *Mary Bell* sure enough."

Yazoo steamed as close to the stricken vessel as the pilot dared and dispatched small boats to help. Fortunately, *Tallahatchie* had tied up between the burning steamer and Point Coupe landing to load cotton aboard *Mary Bell*. Men helped female passengers and children climb aboard *Tallahatchie* while a stiff wind blowing to starboard swept flames away from it. But *Mary Bell* quickly became an inferno. Every deck disappeared in billowing smoke and flames. Several men unable to make it to the gangway jumped overboard, and small boats fished them out.

A man standing next to Jesse timed the fire's progress. When it reached the waterline he announced, "That took less than ten minutes."

Jesse experienced a flush of despair. About three years ago he began a new life aboard that vessel. Jesse felt like a man who left home for many years and returned only to watch his house burn down He lost something irreplaceable that afternoon, and the Colonel recognized its significance.

They remained on the hurricane deck, well apart from the others. After a period of reflection his pensive mentor said something that further depressed the boy's spirits. "That seems to be the fate of our way of life. It is disappearing before us. By the end of the century nothing will remain above the waterline."

"I'm not sure I agree with that."

The Colonel looked at him with an expression that Jesse could not be sure of but may have been sadness. For a few moments he opened up to the boy. "I decided that I would leave my legacy, such as it is, to a young man. I wanted you to pick up where I left off, but it is too late for that. Everything around us is disappearing like tears in rain. Giant tugs now push barges loaded with freight up and down the river. They stop only at cities and towns. Prigs are shutting down gaming parlors along rivers and eliminating gambling on wharfboats. Many wealthy individuals now travel in luxury aboard trains that reach from town to town. Their passage is cheaper, faster, and safer."

The Colonel paused and looked directly at Jesse. "I will stay where I am until the end, and you are welcome to remain with me. However, you must keep in mind that this river is history, and it is changing its course forever." The Colonel hesitated. "I noticed a thick stack of papers in your room with your handwriting. I assume it is your journal, and I am pleased that you took my advice. Continue putting your story on paper. Someday you may want to share it. But be careful about which bridges you cross and which you burn." The Colonel stopped after that observation and retired. Though Jesse did not know it at the time, he would take the Colonel's advice and depart sooner rather than later.

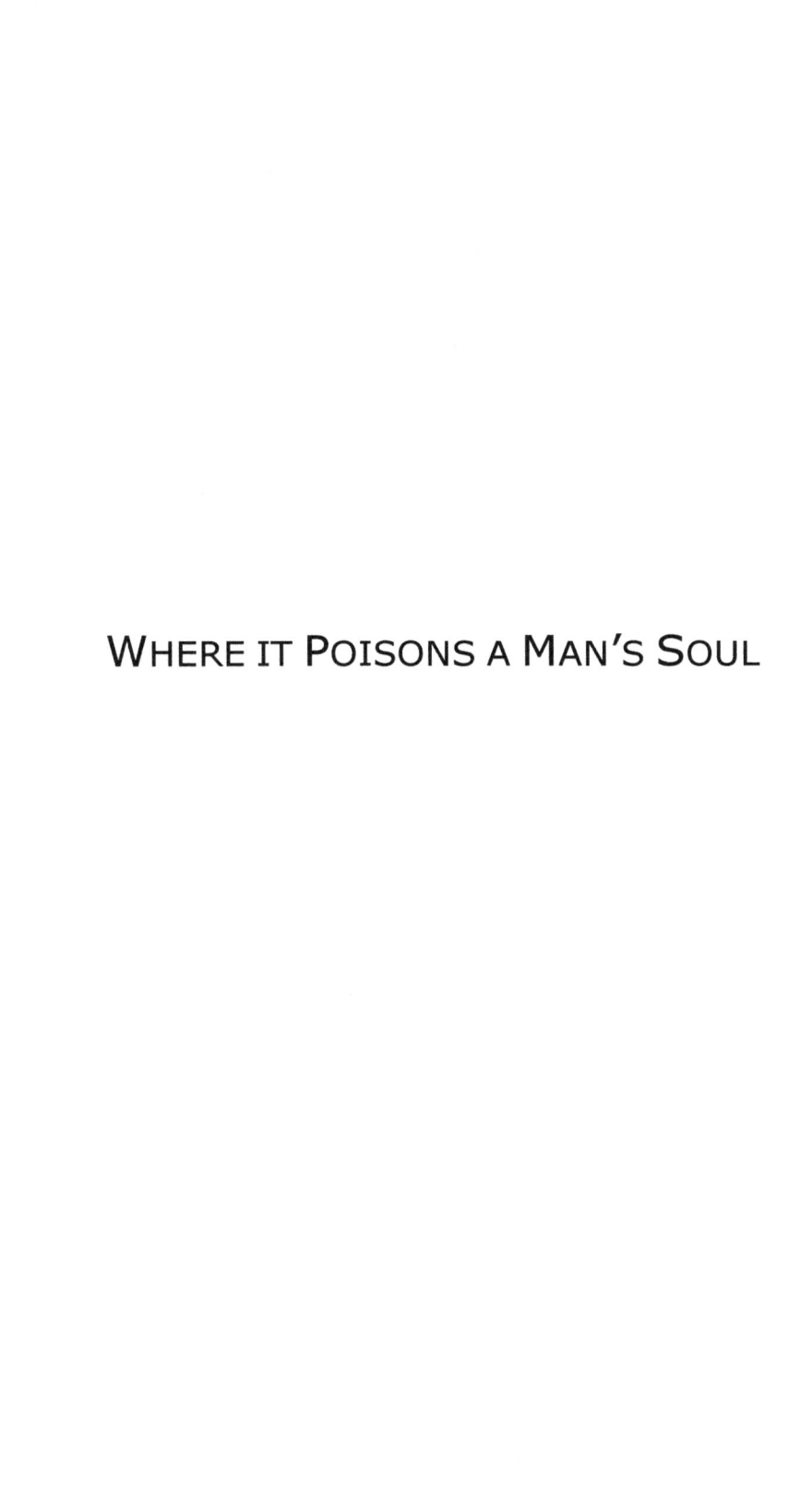

WHERE IT POISONS A MAN'S SOUL

10

Jesse's first vision of her stunned him. He saw Missy Tolliver coming out of the Peabody Hotel in Memphis wearing a pale yellow chiffon dress with a matching hat. She glowed. Perhaps it was the streetlamp illuminating her clothes and blonde hair, or maybe not, but she made a shimmering apparition. Missy turned and smiled at the black doorman as she stepped into the Winston Flyer. During this movement she noticed Jesse nearby, staring at her, and she smiled at him. Her brother Karl didn't own a smile. He wore a sporting cap, goggles, fringed gauntlets, a tan linen suit, and a white shirt with a red ascot that accentuated his pale skin. Karl's face twisted into an arrogant scowl, which appeared to come naturally. After the motorcar pulled away Jesse asked the doorman, "Who was that?"

"That was Mr. Karl Tolliver and his sister Missy. They're from across the river. Their daddy has a big Arkansas plantation over there. Miss Tolliver goes to school over here at a school for young ladies. Mr. Karl comes across now and then for shopping and dinner at Justine's. They go back on their own steamboat with Captain Lawrence Kelly in command."

"Are they going to their steamboat?"

"Reckon so. Both goin' back tonight."

"Is their steamer at the piers?"

The elderly black man's wizened face turned serious. "You best not disturb those folks. Mr. Karl wouldn't like that. Besides, Captain Kelly is down at the docks loadin' convicts for passage across."

"What convicts?"

"Vagrant colored men. Least that's what the law says."

This information caused Jesse to walk into a brisk wind toward the piers to find a way across the river. After asking directions from several stevedores he found the Tolliver steamer and Kelly standing beside it checking off a list of materials being loaded. Hardly five feet tall and skinny with a tan face painted by the sun, he looked up when Jesse approached. "What do you want?"

"A job."

Kelly looked closer. "Have nothing for you." He turned his attention back to the list of shovels, saws, picks, and other items necessary to clear land.

"I know you need help," Jesse said, nodding toward the line of black men being prodded up a gangplank.

"Those are convicts for work clearing ground and helping at our sawmill. You wouldn't last a day there. Besides, we only use colored men for that work."

"I can do any work you have. If I don't you won't have to bring me back here. I'll swim back."

Kelly turned to him. "Boy, you got more talk than a St. Louis lawyer. Why do you want to cross over? Is the law looking for you over here?"

"No, sir. I just want to work over there."

"How did you get to Memphis?"

"I've been working on steamers for about three years."

"Doing what?"

"About everything. Whatever they needed."

"You leave owing them money?"

"No sir. I don't owe anyone anything."

At that point T. R. Cross, a chunky, bald riding boss who oversaw plantation labor, approached them. "What does he want?"

"This boy wants a job across the river and won't take no for an answer. A windy-spinner he is."

"Must be a wooble. Last thing I need is a dimwitted boy," Cross said.

"I'm not dimwitted. I can handle any mathematical problem you have.

Both men frowned. "Have you ever seen anything like this lad?" Kelly asked.

"Can't say I have," replied Cross. "Wonder if anything he says is true."

"It's all true," Jesse insisted.

"What do you want to do with him?" Kelly asked Cross.

"I guess he can fetch and carry 'til he breaks," Cross replied after studying Jesse's size and stout build. "We'll see how fast he talks then." Cross turned to Jesse abruptly. "If you got work clothes you better get them. You'll need them where you're going.

Jesse ran down to his steamer, praying to god all the way that he would not meet the Colonel. God must have heard him because the Colonel was in the saloon running a keno game. Jesse loaded his gear in a sack, put on his roughest cowboy clothes, and wrote a brief note. "Colonel. Thanks for all you did for me, but I have to go. I hope to see you again someday." In his rush to return to the Tolliver steamer, Jesse decided to come back another day to get almost $5,000 he had in a Merchant and Planters Bank safety deposit box.

Jesse soon learned that he owed his new job to a black Baptist minister. Able-bodied black men convicted on trumped-up vagrancy charges had to choose between a chain gang or being leased to plantations. Landlords worked them in awful conditions, but to meet demands for farm labor, officials made chain gangs a worse proposition. Overseers set most convicts free only for their own funerals. Tolliver's riding bosses used wretched methods as well but made the mistake of abusing a Baptist deacon who got word to his pastor about cruel treatment in Arkansas. Memphis authorities enjoyed generous bribes from Beale Street shebang owners, and the deacon's brother owned one and made large donations to the mayor and pastor. Black political support helped the mayor keep a lid on boiling resentment of police brutality. The mayor insisted on the deacon's release and reduced Tolliver's prisoner quota to get the attention of Arkansas planters. This made Cross short of help, and he hired Jesse for a dollar a day plus food and shelter. The job consisted of keeping water cans full and doling out from a tow sack what passed for human food.

After climbing aboard the steamer, Jesse settled on the main deck and felt the gentle, lapping water rock the vessel like a cradle rocks a baby. Then he took stock of what he had done. Somehow her smile had undone him. No thought to the decision and perhaps impossible prospects for success. He broke the Colonel's rules. Yet that smile. There was that smile. He recalled the New Orleans voodoo man's love potion that turned one into a besotted creature. Jesse became angry at himself, but not desperate, like a black man on the steamer. All the prisoners had been shackled together. If the boat sank, all of them would go under with it. The prisoner begged Cross to release him so he could leap into the river and kill himself. Cross said he could kill himself after his sentence ended. During the almost two-hour trip Jesse stared at the boiler deck, the location of staterooms, hoping to see Missy, but she never appeared.

After docking at a plantation landing in Mississippi County, Cross took the reins of his quarter horse from a black man named Ned. The riding boss saw Ned's mutt sitting beside a trailer gnawing a bone and warned Ned. "You don't give that potlickin' dog any food you brought for these men."

"No, sir. I got him some bones in a sack."

Cross shook his head, but the mongrel followed Ned everywhere. Cross then led these shackled men along a corduroy road into the gloomy swamp. Missy and her brother remained in their staterooms until the prisoners marched away. After walking and stumbling a good ways many of the convicts collapsed and begged for water. Though frustrated, Cross directed Jesse to remove water and gruel from the wagon and dole out rations equally. Jesse had been riding in the wagon with Ned, beset by mists of swarming mosquitoes. He took the same portion of water and gruel for himself, but the riding boss interrupted. "You eat all you want. You'll need it where you're going."

"That's enough. I'm not all that hungry."

Cross surveyed the exhausted men and bedded them down for the remainder of the night. When the sun arrived that following morning, Jesse stared at the swamp that surrounded them. The water had a green velvet cover often broken up by cypress trees and thick underbrush. It appeared to go on forever. While holding shotguns at the ready, Cross and Ned ordered the prisoners to rise. "You boys get up!" Cross shouted. "We got a ways to go. You will get those chains off when we get to the work camp. But you got to keep a steady gate so we can get there by noon."

The chain jangled as men stood, but two of them were so weak that others had to help them. They continued at a slow walk often through rancid water sometimes knee high. Ned told Jesse to walk the mules pulling their wagon until they reached firmer ground. This he did while staring at the wilderness. Millions of mosquitoes continued to swarm them, and men attempted to slap them away, but to no avail. Ever so often Jesse saw lethal water moccasins with their fat brown bodies spread along tree limbs waiting for prey. When the line of men approached too near, the vipers raised their upper jaws almost to the back of their necks, a warning not to come closer. As soon as the men reached a narrow dirt road, Ned handed Jesse the reins and taught him how to manage the mules. Though he had never done this before, it turned out to be an easy task since the mules knew what to do without guidance. Jesse merely had to sit on the seat and let them set their pace.

When they reached the labor camp the young man's distress almost overwhelmed him. Most prisoners were at work not far from the camp. Those too weak were held inside cages. The emaciated black men looked to be deathly ill, and some were. They sat on filthy cots infested with vermin. Several had lacerated backs where leather straps had split open large swaths of their skin. Their stripes reeked of infection, with pus seeping out of them. Several manacled men in the column began to moan low. Cross turned toward them. "Shut up or you'll get some of them stripes."

Jesse realized that the surrounding wilderness formed a barrier preventing escape. If a riding boss didn't kill you, the elements would. It being noon, Cross told Ned to draw enough rations to feed the new prisoners and those already at work. Ned helped Jesse take rations from their wagon and strap bags holding the food onto two mules. The riding boss told Jesse to follow him down a path to where men were working. The now unshackled new workers walked and stumbled in front of Cross' horse, and the boy followed him leading two mules. Soon he smelled smoke, and they passed out of the woods into a clearing. Jesse saw prisoners cutting down brush and trees too small for lumber and throwing them onto a fire. Flames rushed upward, and smoke followed. A riding boss at that location, Monroe Parker, grew angry at a convict too weak to handle a log by himself. He stumbled, and Parker's whip found his back. The man cried out in pain and dropped the log, which fell on his leg and broke it. Cross saw it and yelled. "Goddamnit Monroe! Now look what you've done. We can't get any more prisoners, and you're killing the ones we got."

Though Cross outranked the other riding boss it did not stop Parker from confronting Cross so as not lose face in front of these men. "If they won't do their share I don't need 'em. I'll kill 'em all if I have to," Parker shouted.

That night Ned and Jesse bedded down in the wagon and covered themselves with burlap bags to block some of the mosquitoes, but the boy couldn't sleep. "What all is wrong with those men in the cages?" he asked Ned.

"Most of them got the bleedin' trots. They won't last much longer."

After an hour or so of twisting and turning on the wood wagon floor a piercing, eerie sound brought Jesse to his knees. "What is that?"

"Don't be afraid of that whistler. I got my shotgun ready, I'm waitin' on him."

"What's a whistler?"

"Them is big black panthers whistling at timber workers. They want men to come out to see where they are. They can eat a man live. I heard of that."

Jesse gulped and ignored the swarming mosquitoes. "Ned, have you got another gun? I'm a real good shot with a pistol. An expert taught me how."

Ned reached into his tote sack and took out a crude but large hunting knife. "Here's my wade-and-butcher blade. You can skin that bad boy after I kill him. I been wantin' to take on one of them all my life. They used to whistle around our homeplace. My mama and daddy and my brothers and sisters was slaves when I was a waist-baby. We stayed out in the woods up near Wittsburg workin' for Mr. Cyrus. We didn't know we was free after the war. Mr. Cyrus never told us nothin'. He kept all of us away from everybody. Told my mama to stay near our cabin by the 40 acres we worked for him. Said out there was whistlers and rattlers just waitin' on us. We heard they killed a fair amount of colored folks. We didn't know no better until a travelin' preacher, a Bible-thumpin' Baptist, came by the field where we was workin' and asked to share a meal with us. He prayed over that meal 'til the food got cold but told us the war was over two years and we was free. Mr. Cyrus said he'd kill us if we tried to run off, but he caught the fever and couldn't get out of bed. We run off during the night and got away from there." Ned grew silent and pondered his dreadful memories. "Watch out for the spinners out here. The black widow kind can kill you with one bite. Yes they can."

Jesse made it through the night despite Ned's scary creatures and the night sounds they made, and when the young man delivered food to the sawmill he stayed no longer than necessary. Flying chips put out eyes; taut cables came loose and flew through the air, separating human limbs from bodies, and rolling logs crushed arms and legs. Young boys, called dust monkeys, had the most dangerous job. They huddled beneath whirling blades to keep sawdust from building up. Like other prisoners felling trees and clearing underbrush, these men had little chance of paying off their surety debts. Rooster, the sawmill manager, charged them 15 cents for a drink of water and docked them an hour for water breaks. Every week the prisoners grew deeper in debt and unable to pay off their fines and court costs. It was slavery by another name.

Jesse worked as their step-and-fetch-it for about a month before he came down with typhus. It started with severe headaches, fever, and then delirium. Ned and Jesse had formed a comfortable relationship, and the black man knew the boy would pull his weight if possible. But it became impossible, and Ned went to Cross when Jesse couldn't stand up one morning. "Boss, that boy is real sick. He can't go no more. He's gonna die if he don't get help."

The riding boss frowned, clearly aggravated by the news. "I knew I shouldn't have brought that white boy out here. He ain't talking big now is he?"

"He's game as a fightin' cock, but he can't go no more. I can take him back to headquarters on my next trip and bring Lucius back. We can manage all right."

"Hell, Lucius is more trouble than an egg sucking dog." Cross paused, searching for a better idea, but not finding one. "You tell Lucius that if he causes problems I'll put him under the blades with those dust monkeys. And you tell that white boy that when he gets well he has to work. No slacking."

"Yes sir. I'll make sure of that."

Ned took Jesse back to plantation headquarters after a bone-jarring, head-snapping wagon ride. He carried the boy into a long bunkhouse of rough pine used by hired hands and put him in one of about 20 small metal beds on a thin mattress. A cook named Marceline brought him broth for sustenance. Abram, an elderly black man who worked in the big house, helped the boy to a privy and back as well as a small room where Jesse could clean himself using a wash tub.

Fortunately, he was clean when Missy walked in with her mother. Dating back to antebellum days, plantation mistresses saw to the medical needs of those who lived on family property. Deborah Tolliver continued this tradition at River Run, the family's plantation. She was training her daughter in the ways of noblesse oblige, so Missy accompanied her that day. As the young woman sponged Jesse's head with cool water to lower his temperature he blushed. Though he welcomed her touch, Jesse avoided staring into Missy's face poised directly above his.

However, he was able to closely observe Mrs. Tolliver for a few moments and did not like what he saw. She was slender with dark blue eyes that sometimes seemed black and had her brown hair pulled back in a severe look that matched the woman's expression. Taken altogether, she looked cold hearted, but determined to do her duty. Mrs. Tolliver opened her thin lips to say, "I hope you feel better now. You are much improved, according to the doctor. We have one who comes to the plantation at least once each week to check on us. He says you have typhus, but it is abating. But you will need to remain in bed until you are better."

"Thanks, ma'am," Jesse said quietly, wondering what he could do to improve his standing with the Tolliver women.

Mrs. Tolliver showed him a way. "Is there anything we can do for you?"

"I would like something to read if it is not too much trouble."

This startled both Missy and her mother. They looked at each other as if to confirm that they heard the same request. "What do you have in mind?" Mrs. Tolliver asked.

"Something by Dickens."

"How about *Pride and Prejudice*?"

"That is not by Dickens," Jesse replied, avoiding her trap. "It is by Jane Austen, and I have read it."

"Oh. You are correct. I cannot keep my British authors sorted out. We will bring you something."

As Jesse had intended, news of that encounter went directly to the big house and improved his status. That evening for supper Marceline brought him a plate of pork belly and snap beans. "That'll stick to your ribs," she said after handing Jesse the plate. "I covered it with some pink-eye gravy I made from the ham hock. The poke is fresh baked."

The next morning after farmhands left the bunkhouse Missy walked in with a copy of *David Copperfield* and a question. "Who are you?"

"What do you mean?"

"What is your name?"

"Jesse Brody."

"Where are you from?"

"Originally from South Carolina, but I have roamed around for a while. Why do you ask?"

"Because you chose to work out in that horrid swamp with prison labor, but you speak like a gentleman. I assume you are or were. I do not know what you are now. You are a mystery man. Mama is intrigued. So am I. Daddy does not believe us. My brother Karl does not care. So tell me about you."

"That would take a long time. Why are you here rather than at school in Memphis?"

"How did you know that I go to school there?" she asked, surprised that he knew.

"A man told me, but I did not get his name."

Missy grew petulant. "Now you are irritating me."

Jesse smiled, assuming an identity he knew well. "I do not like talking about my past, but it was very different from the present."

"Did you attend university? You sound like it."

"I had a private tutor."

"Are you from a wealthy family?"

Jesse seemed pensive. "I prefer not to talk about that. Maybe some other time. Right now I want to start the Dickens.

Missy accepted his demurral since he appeared to be tired. "I will call on you tomorrow. When you feel well I want to hear your story." With that she left, and Jesse knew that he had set the hook, a phrase he retained from his previous vocation.

During her previous visits Missy had dressed plainly with her hair pulled back and little makeup. The next day she gussied up with makeup and hair done up with ringlets. She was a pretty girl with skin the shade of a peach about to ripen and full lips. Missy was not plump, and not skinny, just nicely filled out. And there was that smile. It carried sunshine into the room. That day Missy wore a black dress with yellow, red and tan flowers. "How much Dickens did you master?" she asked.

"All of it."

"I do not see how that is possible in one day." She paused. "I would ask you for some details, but you would show off and trip me up." She paused again. "Are you ready to tell me who you are? You might as well. Daddy is checking with his friends and business associates in South Carolina and asking them about a prominent Brody family."

"That is a waste of time."

"How come?"

"Brody is not my last name."

Missy flushed. "You lied to me. You said it was."

"No. You asked for my name, and I told you. Jesse is my first name, and Brody is my middle name. I did not provide my last name."

Missy sputtered. "Maybe you did not lie outright, but you certainly misled me. That is not the way of a gentleman."

"Actually, it is my experience that most gentlemen will lie to draw the attention of a beautiful woman."

This time Missy blushed. "Your sweet talk is appreciated, but it will not deter me. Will you tell me your surname?"

"No."

"You are impertinent, and I will not bring you another book tomorrow."

"So you will have a southern belle hissy and punish an ill man."

This caused Missy to retreat. "I cannot come tomorrow. The truth is I have to return to Memphis tomorrow afternoon. I am out of sorts because I was given a Latin assignment and have not done it. I do not like the language and am not any good at it. So I will get a mark down, and Daddy will have a fit."

Jesse smiled. "Bring me the lesson, and I will help you with it."

This startled Missy into open-mouthed disbelief. "Do you speak Latin?"

"I am not entirely fluent, but close."

Missy rose and returned to the big house to get her examination. While there she found her mother. "Jesse has agreed to help me with my Latin assignment."

"Do you think he knows Latin?" she asked suspiciously.

"We shall soon know for sure."

11

Missy soon knew for sure, as did her mother and father. Broadus Tolliver decided to see this mystery man for himself. He sent for Jesse, and they met in the gin office. Though he had some weak trembles, the boy carefully assessed the heavyset man with thinning hair, a simian face, and cold eyes. He judged Tolliver to be treacherous and brutal when crossed---a bully with a rat brain. The planter also proved to be blunt. "Boy, I am told by my daughter and wife that you are bright as sunshine. I need someone like you to help Prescott in the cotton gin. He is a good ginner as to keeping the machinery going but cannot keep the books properly. I will give you a list of the things I need to know, weights, grades, and such, to be included in a weekly report. You will give me a summation that I can depend on to settle up with my neighbors and tenants. We will see where we are at the end of the first week, and if I am satisfied we will come to an arrangement fair to both of us."

Jesse knew that fair by the planter's count would be unfair to him, but he agreed. "I am very good with numbers, Mr. Tolliver, and I will not let you down."

"Well, you won't do it but once. Go ask Prescott to come in here, and we will talk it out amongst us."

One of the things they talked about was Jesse's need to cross the river back to Memphis and get some personal property. After hearing this, the planter became combative. "If you have to make trips to Memphis I don't need you. I can't have a hand galivanting off when I need him here working."

"This is the only time I need to go. It will not be a problem."

"Why do you have to go?"

"I have money held at Merchants and Planters Bank that I need to draw down."

This news softened Tolliver's tone. "Well, I suppose that is a different matter."

"Yes, sir. It is quite a lot, so I need to keep it in one of the desk drawers in here. If I put it in my bunkhouse trunk I will not have it for long."

"That I understand. Prescott, have one of the drivers take him to the ferry landing when it is scheduled to cross the river." Tolliver turned to the boy. "You will have to find your own way back. I don't provide free transportation."

"Yes, sir," Jesse replied, and that was that.

After this meeting Jesse decided to take a closer look at the big house. The large white structure had six pillars with a gray slate roof and trim to match. The three-story center rose much higher than wide, two-story additions on each side. A veranda stretched along the front and sides of the home. Jesse observed that it seemed more like a Mississippi or Louisiana plantation house. Those tended to be more grandiose than Arkansas varieties. He walked up the compressed pea gravel path to the house as far as possible without attracting attention. Jesse looked carefully at the home and decided that one day he would own it.

The boy caught a ferry early in the afternoon and made his way to the bank. After taking $500 from his savings, Jesse shopped for some clothes. This led him to Goldsmiths department store. There he purchased seven outfits---five khaki pants with accompanying work shirts, two black pants and white dress shirts, a dark tie, black vest, and suit coat in case he should need to dress up. He picked out work boots and dress shoes along with socks and cotton drawers to replace his long johns. The underwear and overalls he wore had been bought for him at the plantation store and charged to his account. They were ugly and overpriced, as was the interest charged on his account.

After returning to Arkansas that evening on the ferry, Jesse changed clothes and went directly to the gin.

Jesse soon recognized Prescott's value to Tolliver. The ginner had a knack for taking broken things apart, fixing the problems, and putting them back together in working order. This skill proved critical since gin equipment, particularly the four stands that separated lint from seed, broke down often. Tolliver's gin consisted of a cavernous tin structure filled with large tubes. A hired hand used a huge suction tube to pull cotton out of trailers and send it flying along until it entered the stands. They separated lint from seed, hulls and trash. Lint flowed into a press that packed it into 500-pound oblong blocks which workers tied up with metal bands and webbing. Seed traveled a different route to a bin that stored it for sale. A tube with strong, continuous blasts of air hurled trash and hulls out of the gin and onto a pile that grew so large it sometimes rose above the gin roof.

Jesse found the bookkeeping relatively simple so they made a good management team. Plus, he helped Prescott with repairs and other chores. However, their work soon became extraordinarily challenging due to an unexpected problem. Prescott rushed into the gin office one morning and yelled, "All hell's broke loose in Crittenden County. Some nightriders burned down a gin there and all the cotton trailers. Mr. Tolliver just told me about it. They killed a plantation manager when he got in their way. Most planters over there don't want to take their cotton to a local gin because they're afraid those nightriders will burn it. Mr. Tolliver is having all their cotton brought here for ginning. We are fixing to be covered up with cotton. I am bringing in two crews, one for daylight and one for dark. We got to run 24 hours a day. Mr. Tolliver said he would be right over to talk to both of us about how we can handle it."

Tolliver arrived shortly after Prescott's account. He walked into the gin with a grim expression and hitched up his britches by tugging on his suspenders. "I take it ya'll both know about the situation. We will be helping our friends get their cotton ginned. Now we need to be sure our cotton gets ginned first. Do not forget that. After ours, first come first served, except for the wool-hat boys. Those small farmers come last. Jesse, you need to keep a separate set of books for the planters. The two of us will sort it all out when the time comes."

Jesse broke into the pause. "If we run two crews I can handle the day shift or most of it to give Prescott some rest. If you allow it we can bring bunks into the office and sleep in here. That way we can immediately handle anything that comes up."

Two things about this impressed Tolliver. First, that

Jesse could quickly sort out problems. Second, he had the guts to speak up. The planter agreed. "Those are good ideas. Make it so."

"Do you have any friends you want to go to the front of the line?" Jesse asked.

"Young man, you can count my friends on one hand after you cut off all my fingers."

That ended the meeting, and while watching Prescott send runners to the black quarters to summon workers, Jesse considered why Tolliver wanted a separate set of books. He cheated his tenants and nearby farmers in several ways. He inflated gin charges and bribed cotton graders in Memphis to assign low grades to tenant cotton so he could buy the tenant's share at below market prices. Sometimes the planter had Prescott short a trailer weight and switch cotton to Tolliver's account. Apparently, Jesse surmised, other Mississippi County ginners also cheated and knew the tricks, so Tolliver would have to pay them on the square.

Prescott and Jesse lived and slept in the gin office, occasionally observed by Tolliver, for several days until word came that regulators hired by area planters had run to ground the nightriders and hung them. One virtue of working with Prescott, Jesse quickly learned, had to do with the ginner's knowledge of plantation affairs and gossip. This became important because the boy learned that Missy returned to the plantation most Saturdays to attend church with her family on Sunday mornings. The Tollivers went to a non-denominational service in a church building on the plantation. This became a standard practice after the planter learned that during some services at the Catholic girls school that Missy attended, the priests demanded that rich Christians share their wealth with the poor. They should not succumb to the temptation of luxury since it put their souls in great jeopardy. When Tolliver heard of this practice from another planter whose daughter attended the same school he threatened to move Missy to a different academy. But Deborah Tolliver would have none of that. So Missy attended the plantation church where her father paid the preacher's salary for sermons that validated planter practices and lifestyles.

After Prescott told Jesse this story, that following Sunday the boy dressed up and walked to a copse of trees near the brick church and waited for the Tollivers to arrive and take a front pew in the small brick building. Many of the white hired hands and tenant families attended there as well, dressed in their best Sunday outfits. Black workers worshipped in a toadstool church in an empty barn. A whooping preacher delivered their sermons in a volume that projected his exhortations throughout the plantation. After everyone in the congregation had entered that morning a deacon closed the door. Then Jesse walked in, assuming that the squeaking door would attract attention. It did, and Missy along with others turned to see who had just arrived. Her expression revealed surprise at Jesse's entrance, his gentlemanly appearance, and serious demeanor. After this dramatic performance the young man listened to the preacher's justification for slavery as evidenced in the Bible during a sermon that Jesse found ridiculous. He made it a point to leave as communion began so as not to mingle with parishioners. That following Monday Prescott confided in Jesse that he had become a nagging puzzle to everyone on the plantation. Given Prescott's proximity to his bookkeeper, other employees depended on him to solve the riddle. Jesse played the role of a young Carolina planter effectively with hints and innuendo. He also implied that his exodus had something to do with the tragic death of a young lady. Jesse assumed that this romantic tale would eventually reach Missy and cause her to pursue him for more information. He had decided to withhold his full name from everyone. Given Tolliver's extensive connections throughout the South, more information about his identity might lead to recognition that he had been a gambler and grifter. That would eliminate any chance for closer ties to the family.

As harvest weeks passed, Tolliver assigned more financial responsibilities to Jesse. In recognition of the young man's new standing the planter moved him into one of the many small shotgun houses available to members of plantation management. Gin work declined when early winter rains and cold weather arrived shortly after first picking had concluded. The bad weather caused a deterioration of cotton grades to the point that Tolliver wavered about whether to cancel a second picking. He told Prescott to survey the remaining cotton and decide if it merited being picked again.

Prescott and Jesse drove down plantation roads in a black Ford truck with a wood bed. During these trips, the ginner taught Jesse how to drive and the ins and outs of plantation life. River Run had two types of farm employees, hired hands and tenants. Most tenants farmed on the halves, Prescott advised. Each family worked about 40 acres on the plantation's nearly 20,000 acres. Tolliver furnished them land, seed, mules, tools, and personal furnish from his plantation store.

Jesse learned that Tolliver forced these croppers to grow cotton ginned at his facility. Ginning charges and cost of items purchased at the store usually came to more than the tenant's share of crop proceeds, so many families never got out of debt. The effect of this depressing fact materialized in a cotton patch as snow flurries fell softly on the cold damp ground. Prescott and Jessie drove by a field of second picking, and Jesse asked him to stop the truck. He saw a black family -- man, woman, and their children --

pulling the ragged remnants of cotton from frozen bolls. Their pinched expressions told how cold they were. A young woman pulled a small rusted wagon holding a little boy, and the child wore nothing but a cotton night shirt. His mother had on a thin cotton dress. The man and two older boys wore nothing but overalls and undershirts. While Jesse watched them struggle down the half-mile rows dragging their sacks, the cold wind whipped them. He turned away from the family and asked Prescott, "Does Mr. Tolliver know that these people are out here in this weather? That patch is not worth picking. All of them together will not get 100 pounds out of there before dark." Jesse waited for an answer, and Prescott replied reluctantly. "They're out there because they came up way short paying out at the store. Mr. Tolliver said that folks who didn't come close would have to do enough second picking to work it out. That's the only way the plantation can make any money on this scrapping."

"I doubt they'll make enough out of that field to pay out."

Prescott nodded. "Maybe so, but that is between them and Mr. Tolliver. Don't you say anything to him about it. Some folks are worse off than them."

Jesse leaned against his seat for the ride back to headquarters and realized that Tolliver was a monster and the young man helped feed him. The Colonel once told Jesse that monsters still roam the earth, and many of them look human. But what to do about it. Those thoughts wove a dark blanket that almost suffocated the young man's spirit during the entire night. By daylight he still had no answer except that he should resign and move on. When rot sets in, it destroys gradually, inch by inch, until it ruins all it touches. The next few days his work continued to be excellent, and his attitude remained respectful, but his role in the abuse preoccupied him. Prescott noticed the distance Jesse put between them, and Tolliver picked up on it too.

One chilly afternoon the planter asked his ginner, "Is the young man alright? He seems out of sorts about something."

Prescott suggested that it might have to do with the condition of a colored family picking cotton in the snow. "I don't think he knew what to make of it, Mr. Tolliver."

"Well, I'll talk to him about it. He must appreciate how things have to work here. It's why we prosper."

This concerned Tolliver since he recognized Jesse's potential value to the plantation, and the planter had begun grooming him for a significant future there. Most children of wealthy Delta planters continued the antebellum legacy of not indulging in work of any sort. Karl scrupulously observed this tradition. When not attending Ole Miss he passed much of his time in New Orleans at the family's

Garden District mansion with a quadroon mistress. He lived at the Arlington Hotel in Hot Springs during the racing season. Karl studied literature and considered himself a serious poet who could not be concerned with mundane matters such as making money before spending it.

Though Jesse at first did not recognize the full extent of Tolliver's cynicism, it soon became clearer. The planter invited him to dinner on a Saturday night in the big house. This suggested Tolliver's high opinion of Jesse and boosted his ego. The large dining room made an impressive setting. It had a long, wide oak table that could seat a dozen people or more. An embroidered white tablecloth covered it. A massive, matching sideboard made a serving station. Jesse admired the green wallpaper with flowered prints that appeared to be hand painted. The crystal and silver flatware had British imprints, and over it all hung a magnificent crystal chandelier. Jesse recognized immediately that the dining room equaled or exceeded the best that he had observed in floating palaces. What most interested Jesse was that Missy sat down beside him. He recognized that Tolliver was using his daughter for bait. However, since Jesse was in the trap, he decided to enjoy the cheese. Missy appeared to be nervous and stared straight ahead while she ate sparingly. Deborah Tolliver steered the conversation between literature and history, which bored her husband. He asked Jesse about rice production in South Carolina, and

Jesse's detailed answers bored the two women. The young man provided thoughtful answers to all of their questions on a variety of subjects.

The courses began with she-crab soup and ended with a delicious caramel custard for dessert. Jesse praised the meal and thanked the family for their invitation. Before the young man could thank his hosts and depart, Tolliver scooted his chair away from the table and pounced. "Let's go into the study and have a chat and a Cuban cigar. They are excellent."

Jesse agreed, recognizing that they soon would reach the point of his invitation. He nodded to Missy, thanked Mrs. Tolliver for the fine meal, and followed her husband into the study and took a chair proffered by the planter. While Tolliver rummaged through the cabinet holding his cigars, Jesse surveyed the room. Bookcases filled with expensive, leather-bound volumes flanked a red brick fireplace. A painting of Tolliver with a formidable expression filled space above the fireplace. Jesse doubted that the planter had read any of the books and planned to borrow several. A flagstone hearth extended well into the room and led to a massive oak desk where Tolliver spent most of his days. The decorator, presumably Deborah Tolliver, had spaced several plush leather chairs throughout the room, and Jesse took one directly across from the planter. After they lit up their cigars Tolliver began. "The first thing I want to say is how much I appreciate your work. You will find a salary increase in your Friday envelope."

"Thank you," Jesse replied. "I appreciate that. I'm honored to be working for you."

"You'll find this expression of appreciation only the first sign of your future here." Tolliver seemed slightly uncomfortable about pay raises and changed the subject. "I believe you were distressed about what you recently observed in a field of second picking. You must understand our longstanding attitude about workers who are not up to snuff. All they have to do is hold a plow in a furrow and stare at a mule's ass or drag around a cotton sack in the dirt. We must insist that they meet their responsibilities or hired help will take advantage of our concern for their wellbeing. They are like children. They must be punished for bad behavior. If you stay in the Delta you will understand this. It can't be helped."

Tolliver continued with the history of Delta planter relations with negro workers since the Civil War. His remarks consisted of what the Colonel called twisted history, but Jesse inhaled it along with cigar smoke. When he observed a puff of smoke rising, Jesse noticed that the small, shuttered windows blocked most of the sunlight. The young man avoided challenging the planter's version, since it would be wasted words. When time came for them to part,

Tolliver assumed that he had a dedicated believer, and in some ways he did.

12

Jesse decided to play the planter with what the Colonel called a long game. He would win small until the pot got big. This decision would serve him well, since the months ahead required patience and gradual advances. Tolliver assigned Jesse the gin office as his permanent workspace and additional duties with plantation store financial affairs and supervisory issues. The boy saw clearly the venality of his boss. Store prices increased dramatically for those who shopped on credit. Interest carrying costs on accounts reached usurious levels. The plantation paid employees in company scrip for use only at the plantation store, and they were forbidden to shop elsewhere. Few people could pay their bills entirely at harvest time. Since the store provided only annual account summaries, its customers could not verify their accuracy. Many workers could neither read nor write so they lacked the ability to compare their records against store accounts. Those who complained were thrown off the plantation and dumped on a country road by a deputy sheriff. Corruption reached a scale that appalled Jesse, but he went along to get along with Tolliver and cash the planter's increasing pay checks. Sometimes the young man attempted to equate cheating these people with gaming suckers. But he could not forget that slickers mostly cheated punters attempting to cheat them. Helpless tenant families deserved better. It concerned him, but not enough to compromise his rise in the plantation hierarchy. The power seduced him. And there was Missy, who he planned to seduce eventually.

This opportunity disappeared when Missy became engaged and shortly thereafter married Duke Carlton, a young blood who attended Ole Miss with her. He had been a friend of Karl for many years, which led to an inevitable introduction. Missy's parents approved the match since the Carlton plantation, Four Oaks, equaled or exceeded their holdings. Being the oldest son, Duke would rule the empire when his time came. Jesse saw Carlton during his many visits to River Run to spark Missy. He had curly black hair, well oiled, a square jaw, and husky build. Jesse realized that he would have to find a way to alter the odds. Her wedding took place in an Episcopal church in Memphis followed by a gala in the Peabody Hotel banquet hall. Regional high society attended, but Jesse did not since he lacked an invitation. After the lavish party, Missy and her husband departed for New Orleans to sail from there to Rio for a South American honeymoon. During the afternoon of the wedding, Jesse sat in his office and assessed this inconvenient turn of events. For months after his convalescence the young man rarely saw Missy except at church, and she no longer noticed his dramatic entrance. He sensed that she had chosen to distance herself, perhaps on her own, or at the insistence of her parents. Regardless, he had to bide his time and wait for an opening.

Late one afternoon after Missy's wedding, Karl walked into the gin office with an arrogant smile stretched along his thin lips. Karl's viper eyes, hooded and menacing, made Jesse uneasy. Karl reeked of alcohol and slurred a sentence. "Well, Missy is now married to a man worthy of her. That must disappoint you. My father says you are becoming indispensable to plantation operations, and I understand that you charmed and fascinated my sister during your recuperation. But Missy is beyond your grasp now, and when I take over the plantation you will be fired immediately." Karl paused before leaving. "Enjoy this office while you can because it is only temporary."

Jesse learned from Prentiss that Tolliver often needled Karl about his wastrel ways compared to Jesse's work ethic, and this poisoned the water between them. Jesse's enemy had fully revealed himself and violated the Colonel's rule that an adversary should never reveal his strength or position until time to strike. It could be a dangerous mistake.

Jesse always toed the company line even when it led to dreadful results, and his poker face hid his contempt for Tolliver. His deception led to a major promotion after several years of service for the family. Roger Stevens, the long-time farm manager, saved enough money to buy a hill farm in Central Arkansas and raise cattle. After a lengthy discussion with Jesse, Tolliver gave him an opportunity to run the plantation's day-to-day operations, including supervision of several vicious riding bosses. Karl became furious, having failed to talk his father out of the promotion. During that confrontation he learned that his father would never allow paternity to trump profit.

Tenant contracts became one of Jesse's first responsibilities. With his feet propped up on the desk he thumbed through the current version used with all tenants. They had to plant what Jesse told them to, which meant fencerow-to-fencerow cotton at 50 percent crop rent. Cotton must be hauled in Tolliver's wagons to his gin. Tolliver had first rights to purchase the cotton at prices consistent throughout the region---consistent defined by him. Ginning costs would be deducted from sale proceeds. Though the plantation store provided farm inputs and personal provisions on account, the contract mentioned no terms, including an interest rate applied to account balances. Tolliver had the right to seize crops at any time during the year if the planter deemed a farmer's work unsatisfactory.

The plantation carried contracts over from year to year unless the planter elected to modify or cancel them. The year Jesse became manager he had a table placed on the concrete floor in a large area of the gin. After evaluating the work of tenants and farm hands with Cross, Prescott, and Tolliver, Jesse reluctantly sent word to those who would be thrown off the plantation. The 20 or so families arrived and huddled together in a corner like hunted creatures on the African veldt. The men had little to wear but coveralls over long johns. Most women had on calico dresses over long johns. Many of their children wore shirts made from empty flour sacks and pants made from burlap bags. Jesse avoided eye contact with the men he called forward. He handed each one any cash the family had coming from crop proceeds in excess of their store accounts. Sometimes when men walked back to their family and showed their wives the meager sum the women would cry out. They had lost everything, with no place to go and nothing to take with them. When Jesse looked at them, the fear in their eyes and their weeping children increased the shame he felt, so he stopped looking. After he paid off the last family, a thin, grief-stricken wife walked up to him and said quietly, "Now that you're done and can't hurt us no more, I'll speak my mind. We may not know where we're going now, but I know where you're going sooner or later. Old Scratch is saving a place in hell for you, and you're going there fast. What you're doing may do to live by, but it won't do to die by."

Jesse accepted her warning silently but recognized that at some point he had come to a fork in the road and turned the wrong way. His reverie ended when Abram limped into the cavernous space. "Mr. Jesse," the arthritic old man said. "Mr. Cross told me I'm gettin' throwed off. I got nowhere to go but in the St. Francis River. I got to walk in and not walk out. He says I got too many deducts to stay. I don't know what all them are. I can't live on the rations I get. I been pullin' turnips and tater grabbin' at night, but still don't have enough to eat. What am I gonna do if I get throwed off?"

Jesse had known Abram ever since the young man crossed the river. This kind, gentle black man helped him endure typhus and regain his health. Jesse recalled many instances of support and decided that he would break a plantation rule. "Abram, in the morning you tell Percy to give you what food you need. That I said so. I'll tell Cross to leave you alone, that you are going to help me with things around here."

Jesse saw the man's tears when Abram spoke. "I'll praise you to the Lord this Sunday."

"It may be a bit late for that, but I suppose it can't do any harm."

"No sir. The Good Lord never gives up on folks. His amazin' grace saves us all."

"I hope you are right," Jesse replied as he escorted Abram out the door. It was the only thing Jesse felt good about in a long time, though the decision meant little. It was like trying to bail out a sea of misery with a small bucket.

The day's crises did not end with Abram. After him, Rooster came in and began his complaint. "We can't grind any more corn cause the lazy tom is tore up. Arthur Gene broke it when he was tryin' to fix it. I can't get it goin' again."

"Why did you let him go near the damn thing?"

"When I went to get me a glass of buttermilk from Pearl he wasn't messin' with it. When I got back he was studyin' it real careful, but it won't work no more."

"Call Memphis and get that repair man over here. Tell Arthur Gene to make himself scarce because he better not run into me."

Rooster put on his straw hat and replied, "Yes sir. I'll tell him, but I don't think he wants to run into you no how."

Jesse took on many onerous responsibilities, including long-distance oversight of a cotton mill south of Helena owned by Tolliver's plantation, Sunnyside plantation, and Red Leaf plantation. Jesse had never been there and only counted the money that came in from its operations. He tried to explain to Tolliver that he could not verify accuracy of the split without going there. Jesse would have to look things over and establish a method to monitor income and expenses. Even then, if skillful cheating existed, Jesse had little chance of discovering it. But Tolliver insisted on an inspection. On the way to his car Jesse heard a rain crow's warning and returned for his umbrella. While heading south in a company car with its windshield wipers slapping a squeaky beat, Jesse passed slowly through Helena. He experienced a rush of melancholy while observing changes in the town and a scarcity of boats at the piers. It seemed that the decaying port no longer shared his memories. After a two-hour drive south, the young man came upon a sign posted where the highway intersected with a private gravel road.

It warned in tall bold letters: BARTON COTTON MILL.VISITORS NOT WANTED OR ALLOWED. Jesse drove down the gravel road until he reached the mill, which had a high wood fence surrounding it. The facility employed women and children, and while passing a long row of shacks he saw babies crawling on the steps and in the road. Their hands had been tied up with cloth, and their wrists and arms had ugly sores. Their mothers and older sisters worked from

5:45 a.m. to 6:30 p.m. with a 30-minute lunch break. When Jesse pulled up to a small tin building with an office sign a short, obese man with sweat pouring down his pale bald head waddled out to meet him. The manager knew of Jesse's arrival due to a telephone call, but clearly did not expect such a young man to emerge from the car. "Mr. Brody?" he asked, unsure if he had the right person.

"Yes, Mr. Carter, glad to meet you." Jesse held out his hand to shake with Carter and found a clammy palm that felt like a dead carp. Carter's body odor also made a disagreeable impression. It traveled with him like moisture in a dark cloud. Jesse decided to separate himself from Carter as soon as possible. "I noticed driving in that small children outside company housing had a lot of sores and scabs on them. Has there been an outbreak of some disease?"

"No. We got a mosquito plague."

"Has any action been taken to combat the mosquitoes?"

"No, but we told all these women to keep their kids inside."

Jesse had noticed that the unpainted, rough-hewn labor houses lacked window screens and proper ventilation, which made that recommendation useless. "I gather from talking to you by phone that the workers here are Italian women and children. Do any men work here?"

"No. Only women and children sent up here by the Chicot County plantations. Our work requires little fingers, not big hands."

Carter led Jesse on a tour of the working area. Children stood nervously in front of enormous machines, their little fingers winding in and out among large skeins. Strained, tired eyes nervously watched thin arms carefully guiding the thread to avoid a mistake that would cause their pay to be docked. Jesse noticed that a girl standing near him wearing only a cotton shift had stunted limbs and a deathly pale face, reflecting her fear of reduced wages. He turned to Carter and shouted over the noise of whirling machinery. "Take me to the office. I need to go through your records."

This Carter did with some trepidation, and Jesse located himself upwind of Carter and in front of the lone fan struggling to push away hot air. After several hours Jesse determined that he could never sort out the mill's financial affairs unless he stayed a few days each week, which he would never agree to do even if it cost him his job. The young man packed his notes in a briefcase, said goodbye to Carter from upwind and headed home.

Shortly after his arrival Tolliver found him in the gin office and sank into a large leather wing chair opposite the desk. "Well, what do you think?"

"What I think is that the only way we can know for sure if financial impropriety exists is to hire an experienced bookkeeper and send him down there until he can answer that question. It would cost us a lot of money, and it may not turn up anything. Short of that we might as well cash the monthly checks and hold off unless there is an unexplained shortfall in our share of mill income. I do not mean to be disrespectful, but you pay me for honest answers, and that is my honest answer. We do need to consider putting screens on windows in labor houses down there. Mosquitos are causing major problems."

"Are they hurting our workers?"

"No, mostly their children."

Tolliver rose from his chair. "I'll sleep on it," he said, but never mentioned the subject again.

13

One of Cross' responsibilities required him to attend county court on Monday mornings to pay fines levied on black workers convicted of vagrancy. The number of these arrests varied, depending on the needs of area plantations since prisoners had to work out their debts to planters who paid their fines. Cross broke two ribs when his horse skittered and threw him to avoid a rattler, so Tolliver assigned Jesse the task. Dejected black men walked into court shackled, and some attempted to explain that they had jobs, but a justice of the peace interrupted and found them guilty. Riding bosses and farm managers looked on and competed to pay fines of men known to be good workers. Jesse knew that planters set wages at only 85 cents a day so he should bring home a few men to replace those who died at the sawmill and or tree-clearing crews. The young man paid their fines, and a deputy sheriff agreed to deliver them to River Run.

The plantation's labor problems peaked when World War I began in Europe during August 1914. Several crop exchanges failed to open, and cotton prices fell by about ten dollars per bale. Though Tolliver could now buy cotton cheap, he had to sell it cheap as well. The planter fumed and put pressure on Jesse to solve this problem. Tolliver demanded that the young man assess the plantation's cotton inventory and purchase commitments and devise a proposal. Their meeting to discuss this was held in the big house study, and Tolliver became livid while hearing Jesse's report about the situation.

"What do you plan to do? I pay you good money to handle problems like this, and I don't see you handling it. This could break me," Tolliver growled.

Jesse did not share his first impression when charged with this failure. It being that he lacked the authority to prevent European wars. However, he proposed a strategy that if successful would produce handsome profits rather than ugly losses. Jesse had become the region's high priest of finance, knowing when to add and when to subtract and when to open and when to close. "I have thought about this a great deal, and one approach worth considering has risk, but worthwhile rewards. Right now the cotton we are holding is our share or tenant shares that we purchased cheap. So why sell it now at a loss. If America enters the war, which is likely, the value of cotton will soar. It will be needed for uniforms, and we will benefit from much higher prices."

Tolliver stopped fuming long enough to mull over the consequences. "What about all the cotton we have contracted to buy. We have no profits to purchase it, and we will have to borrow the cash to cover our contracts."

"Not necessarily," Jesse replied. "We just renegotiate our contract terms so that we control the bales but do not have to purchase them until a future date. Producers are so strapped for cash that we can offer a small advance to close the deal. Our gin storage will accommodate the contracted bales. If we hold them long enough and America enters the war, we close on all the inventory and reduce the price by charging high storage fees. Contract language will be vague on that issue. Naturally, we will reduce the price by advances given. Since this inventory will fetch higher prices, owners will be less likely to kick."

"What if we don't enter the war? What happens then?"

"We sell our holdings, probably at a price no worse than today's spot offers."

"We may lose some tenants and local farm customers if that happens," the planter warned.

"True, but that is their problem, not ours. We can replace them easy enough. Tenants without farms will be filling country roads all over the Delta. We can hire all we want at our price, not theirs."

Tolliver agreed with the plan, and fortunately for Jesse, America entered the war in April 1917. The planter got richer, but the family faced another problem. One morning Tolliver found Jesse at the plantation's grain bins measuring the amount of corn stored. As usual he came directly to the point. "I suppose you've not yet heard the bad news."

"What news?" Jesse asked, setting aside the long copper probe used to gauge the depth of grain.

"Duke died in some place called the Ardennes several days ago. Missy just now got the telegram. I told that damn fool to stay out of the war, but he wanted to march off in a pretty new uniform and impress everyone. What is worse, he didn't die a soldier's death, an honorable one. He died of something called the Spanish flu. Not one good thing has ever come out of Spain. All those boys do is dress up like sissies and stick swords in cows. Duke should have stayed home and worked on having a son." Tolliver paused. "I'm going to Four Oaks tomorrow to see Missy and help with things. I want to make sure she gets what is coming to her. The Carltons will cheat her if they can. Those bastards are a pack of thieves." Amid Tolliver's exit he stopped and turned toward Jesse. "I suppose now you know why I refused to let you join the army. Of course, I didn't have to stand in Karl's way due to what he and his mother call a bone spur, whatever the hell that is. We both know that my son is soft as a fluffed pillow." Tolliver ambled off, his face as pink as a spanked baby, and Jesse experienced sinful pleasure in hearing of Duke's death. He considered it a fortuitous development and continued to measure the grain.

Jesse received an invitation to the funeral in the Carlton plantation's Episcopal church and burial in the family cemetery located nearby. He sat in a back pew and walked alone to the gravesite. After the priest closed with a prayer, mourners threw a handful of dirt on the coffin. Jesse stood well away from the grave, and while family and friends walked toward the mansion bracketed by four ancient oak trees, Jesse strolled among the tombstones. Many had names carved in them followed by C.S.A. and an 1860s date. Freshly cut flowers adorned each gravesite, and manicured, vivid green grass surrounded them. The scene was southern to its core. It reminded Jesse that southerners would never let go of the past because it birthed and nourished their pretensions. By the time Jesse entered the cavernous great hall the reception was underway and crowded. He took a glass of punch from a server and found a place to lean against the wall and observe the goings on. The coarseness of what he saw surprised him.

A string quartet played a discreet dirge as people milled about. Missy appeared to be miserable while enduring a flood of condolences. Duke's college chums sipped punch spiked with whisky from their monogrammed silver flasks. After a few glasses they seemed especially drawn to Mrs. Carlton. Tall, with a snow-white complexion and striking red hair, she welcomed their attention graciously, a bit too much so Jesse believed. Mr. Carlton, a short, bald, corpulent man, looked as useless as Napoleon at Elba. All of this occurred beneath the watchful eyes of Carlton ancestors staring down from portraits spaced along the walls in wide gilded frames. Mrs. Tolliver moved from one group to another with her normal poise and desert dry expression, but Jesse suspected that she was appalled by the spectacle. Mr. Tolliver had cornered several prominent planters who appeared uninterested despite his torrent of oratory about gathering more boodle for their bank accounts.

After becoming bored with it all and unwilling to lie to Missy about his sorrow, Jesse walked back to his car parked by the church and returned to River Run. He knew that Missy saw him from where she sat during the priest's brief graveside remarks, but Jesse would approach her only after a respectable period of mourning. That would be awhile. After one week at River Run she departed for New Orleans to travel with her spinster Aunt Marion for a few weeks.

The shortage of laborers during the war caused a collateral problem for planters. Many black men joined the army and marched off to serve in Europe. Their relatives who remained at home received government checks, which made them less likely to work for poor wages. This situation incensed Tolliver, who lobbied a senator to delay the checks until winter, when planters didn't need much farm labor. Despite haranguing Senator Fredericks during a phone call, the planter learned that payments would not be delayed. The senator explained that postponing financial assistance to relatives of men fighting oversees would not be supported by any politician anywhere. Fortunately for Jesse, the planter did not blame him for higher wage costs due to the war. He noticed that Tolliver rarely criticized him for anything after Missy returned to River Run. The young man sometimes saw her pulling weeds among azaleas and rose bushes in the plantation garden during good weather and occasionally when he met Tolliver in the planter's study to discuss business matters. She purposely avoided him, and Jesse attributed this to Missy's recognition of her diminished value in plantation culture. No longer a young beauty, though still attractive, she had almost reached the outer limit of childbearing age. Jesse still wanted her as much as ever but decided to bide his time until he spotted a tell. It came during fall when gin pipes rattled day and night. Late one afternoon while Jesse pored over gin records he looked up to see her in the doorway holding a tray covered by a linen cloth. "If you are here to apply for a job you need to talk to Prentiss. I am not hiring."

"What a tease you are, Mr. Brody, or whatever your name is." He noticed that Missy was well turned out with a new hairdo. "Daddy said you were at it day and night and probably would appreciate a decent meal. I brought you some of Pearl's chicken and dumplings, cornbread, sweet potato casserole, and pecan pie. It is scrumptious."

"Thanks. I've been living on peanut butter and jelly sandwiches for a week. That is all Prentiss and I know how to cook. Please take a seat and join me. I need the company. I would offer you some of this coffee, but it is awful and cold."

Missy took a seat and smiled as Jesse uncovered the food, and he noticed her amused expression. "What?" he asked.

Missy giggled. "Do you know that you have cotton lint all over your hair?"

"No, but it has probably been there for several days. The air is full of it. This is not the place to impress a pretty woman." He looked directly into her eyes, but she would not reciprocate. However, he sensed that the remark pleased her. "Do you want some of this food?"

"No, I ate with daddy and mama."

After a chat about the weather, cotton yields, and other innocuous matters, she said goodbye with a smile. Her visit seemed promising. Most eligible young bloods never called on her at River Run, and Missy rebuffed a few ne'er-do-wells who approached. Her daddy called them all talk and no cotton. Still, Jesse could not decide where he fit in. He knew Tolliver considered his daughter a depreciating asset and badly wanted a grandson, but Jesse lacked a Delta pedigree, which he took to be a necessity for approval by Missy's parents. And Karl hated Jesse with such intensity that he would do anything to block his path to acceptance by the Tollivers.

After Missy returned to River Run the planter expressed growing irritation that Jesse would not disclose his family background. Tolliver assumed it shone with some luster given Jesse's personal qualities and education, and it might solve his nagging problem of a widowed daughter with dwindling prospects. Plus, it might give him a grandson.

During a rainy evening as they sat in Tolliver's study the planter cleared his throat and brought up the subject again. "When will you tell me who you are? You can trust me with that knowledge, and you owe it to me."

Jesse pondered his words carefully before responding. "With all due respect, sir, what I owe you is a good day's work for an honest wage. And that you get every day. You hired who I am, not who I was. And that is the end of the matter."

Shocked by this bluntness, Tolliver backed down. "I suppose you are right, but it sticks in my craw that you refuse to tell me more."

"Well, on several occasions you have called me your mystery man. So it is and will always be. Now please look at this list of tenants that I believe we need to let go before next year."

Though Jesse attempted daily to accelerate his relationship with Missy, it came to a standstill when word arrived of an insurrection by black workers near Helena. Jesse walked into Tolliver's office one morning to discuss financial matters, but his boss was on the phone. When Jesse turned to leave, Tolliver motioned that he should take a seat. The planter continued his conversation with a Tennessee planter. "A group of negroes down there have formed a union and plan to attack white planters and steal their property. They shot dead a railroad agent and wounded a deputy sheriff. I made arrangements with sheriffs and county judges to hang the leaders after some trials, but the whole thing is getting out of control." Tolliver paused, listening to the man on the other end of the line. "What you can do now is stop those Tennessee peckerwoods from crossing the river and making matters worse. That ignorant white trash needs to go home and let us handle this. All of us over here have agreed to stop this union business my way, and I will, but these white-cappers are scaring off and killing negroes we need to make our crops. We got to get hold of this situation so I can make an example of the union troublemakers and not run off our help." Tolliver paused to listen before he continued. "I appreciate that Clarence, but I don't want to hire outsiders to handle this. I have the right man for the job, and I am sending him down there. I will keep you informed."

Tolliver interrupted Jesse's reflections. "That conversation never leaves this office. Do you understand me?"

"Yes, sir."

"I am getting a lot of calls from planters about what is going on down there, and I am not sure they know what the hell they are talking about. I need you to go down there and take a hard look and sort it out. And check on the cotton mill. Make sure what is going on in Helena does not have a chance of spreading up here."

Jesse spoke up. "All of the mill workers are Italian immigrants, women and children. Most only speak Italian. I doubt they will make trouble."

"That may be, but we need to know what is happening down there, so go find out."

This order irritated the young man, but he hid his feelings about the venture. After lunch Jesse packed his bag with extra clothes and drove off. As he assumed, peace reigned at the mill, but not in Helena. Jesse drove down main street amid armed white men massed into a large mob. He met Charles Gilliam, a local planter and friend of Tolliver, in the town marshal's office. "What is going on?" Jesse asked the marshal after the lawman finished a telephone call to the governor.

"What is going on," the marshal said, "is we got about a thousand men here from all over. They're fixin' to hunt down and kill these troublemakers."

Jesse studied the tall marshal's flushed face and noticed occasional locks of black hair spread out on his scalp in a ridiculous attempt to hide his baldness. The large man looked mean and formidable. "Are the negroes armed?" Jesse asked.

"Damn right they are. They shot one of my men and killed another. Have Gilliam give you a tour. He knows where all the action is."

"Come on," Gilliam urged, "my truck is outside. We'll start at the Franklin place. There is a crew out there now hunting down a pack of them."

Gilliam drove down a dirt road to the edge of a thicket where a large number of armed white men stood. They were firing into the thicket from both sides to force black men out of cover. Jesse saw about a dozen unarmed men come out holding up their hands to surrender. The mob shot them down. He turned to Gilliam. "None of those men were armed. Why were they shot?"

"We're going to clean house down here, get rid of all the troublemakers." Gilliam drove Jesse down dirt roads made by compacted gumbo soil, and the young man observed several groups of armed men looking for so-called troublemakers. Along a few roads Jesse saw the bloated bodies of dead men and women, and he grew increasingly disgusted.

When Gilliam drove back into town they witnessed hundreds of soldiers setting up 12 machine guns to protect white citizens from supposedly marauding black union members. "Has anyone seen armed negroes attack any white people?" Jesse asked Gilliam.

"We got first-hand testimony. I'll take you to the schoolhouse, and you can see for yourself." After Gilliam parked in front of a three-story brick building two armed soldiers let them in. Jesse heard screams after he walked through the door. The large auditorium held deputy sheriffs, soldiers, and town officials. An elderly black man was tied to an electric chair. When he denied their accusations, the switch sent waves of electricity through his body. The man shook and screamed and struggled against the leather straps to no avail. His interrogator repeated allegations until the man agreed that they were true. "Get me out of here," Jesse ordered Gilliam. After they walked outside, the planter offered to drive Jesse to other locations where men were being questioned, but Jesse declined. "Please take me back to my car." This Gilliam did, while reciting all the events he had witnessed. After Jesse thanked the planter and said goodbye, he drove to a drugstore and dialed Tolliver from a pay phone. "It's me," Jesse said when Tolliver answered.

"What have you found out."

"The threat of a union uprising is apparently a rumor if not a fabrication. It is difficult to separate the two down here."

"Did those negroes start it?"

"Some of them definitely formed a union, or so the man said who drove me around, but I don't know what else they did."

"Are our men taking care of the union hooligans?"

"Yes, they are killing them."

"How many have they killed?"

"It is hard to say. They are killing them faster than you can count them." Jesse paused for a moment. "I am coming home. The mill is not in any danger, and there is nothing to be done here."

"Is there any chance of that insurrection spreading?"

"I can't see how. There will not be anyone alive to spread it."

14

Jesse's worries increased as torrential rains, what Tolliver called toad stringers, continued the following year. Jesse and Cross supervised men piling sandbags on levees for reinforcement. Karl pretended to direct their efforts as well, but mostly pranced around in hand-tailored safari outfits spouting unreasonable demands. Workers generally ignored him and did what Jesse said, which infuriated Karl. When told about water spilling over a levee about two miles from headquarters, he demanded that Jesse drive him to the spot.

"Karl, that is dangerous business. We have overflow ditches to catch the water. If the levee breaks we don't want to be anywhere near there. It may not stop until it hits the secondary levees."

This lecture irritated Karl. "Will you go with me or do I have to go by myself and do your job for you?"

This amounted to showing off in front of the hired help, but Jesse could not let it pass without losing face. "I'll take you down there, but this is unnecessary, and you may regret it." Jesse took some comfort in assuming that Karl would go up the road a ways, become scared, and order him to turn around. After sloshing down a slick gumbo road for a couple of miles, Jesse saw water racing over the top of a levee.

After he stopped the truck, Karl laughed nervously and goaded him. "Pull up some more so we can get a closer look, unless you are afraid to."

"That is not a good idea. We can get in a lot of trouble here."

"Well get out and wait while I drive closer." Karl's vanity had outrun any common sense he possessed.

"I'll pull up some more, but then we are turning around."

Jesse drove closer to the potential washout but had no chance to turn around. The levee disintegrated, and rushing water hit the pickup broadside like a tidal wave. The truck flipped onto its side and was swept along by rushing water. When Jesse came to his senses, he realized the impossibility of escaping through the driver side window since mud and debris blocked it. After kicking the front window several times, it shattered and Jesse climbed out and jumped away from the sliding vehicle. He had not given any thought to Karl's predicament and was unable to help him since racing water carried the truck in one direction and him in another. Jesse eventually worked his way out of the debris-filled gusher into standing water formed by a secondary levee and watched the truck lodge on a high dob. He waded toward the vehicle and eventually reached it. Pinned beneath the crushed-in dash, Karl died with his head under the muddy water. Jesse pulled on his arms to dislodge the body but lacked the strength to free Karl. After recognizing the futility of attempting to retrieve Karl's body, he walked toward plantation headquarters and came upon a tenant driving his tractor pulling a trailer with the family's meager possessions. Jesse hitched a ride.

Cross saw Jesse coming and raced toward him in a farm truck. "Where's Karl?" he asked.

"Down the road with a pickup on top of him. He drowned."

"Goddamnit! Are you sure he's dead?"

"Yes, but you need to take one of the large tractors down there with a few men and try to get him out of the truck. I will go tell Mr. Tolliver."

Badly bruised, covered with mud and limping from a stove up knee, Jesse walked to the big house and knocked on the door. Missy answered. "What happened?" she asked after digesting her shock at his appearance.

"You need to get your mother and father."

"Do you want to come in?"

"No. Not like this."

Missy rushed away and soon returned with her parents. They looked at Jesse with dismay and apprehension. "What happened?" Tolliver asked brusquely.

"The levee broke by the Howerton farm, and Karl did not make it out of the truck."

Deborah Tolliver made a fist and held it to her mouth, Missy gasped, and Tolliver raged. "What the hell were you down there for with the river this high? That was a damn fool thing to do."

Jesse chose a conciliatory tone. "That is what I told Karl, but he disagreed and demanded that I take him." Jesse stood on the porch while the Tollivers took it in. "I tried my best to lift the truck off him, but I couldn't. It was too heavy."

"Is anyone going after him?"

"Yes. I sent Cross and some men."

"I will change clothes and get my waders. Wait on me."

"Yes, sir."

Deborah Tolliver and Missy glanced at Jesse before turning their backs and walking away.

Karl's body came back to the plantation headquarters covered by a wagon tarp amid the bowed heads of people who stood around Tolliver. Fortunately, several men heard Jesse's repeated warnings to Karl and his attempts to discourage the venture. They told Tolliver this and confirmed that Jesse had practically begged Karl not to go. This insulated Jesse from the planter's wrath.

The funeral home returned Karl's body in a plush copper casket and opened it in the big house's expansive hallway. Before family, close friends and dignitaries arrived to pay their respects, Tolliver sent for Jesse. They met in the study. The young man stood while Tolliver sat down on a leather couch and slumped forward before speaking. "I want you to know that I do not blame you for any of this. Everyone says you tried your best to talk Karl out of it." The planter paused and reflected. "Cross says it took six men to lift the truck enough to get the body out. You can't be blamed for that either. It is just one of those things." Tolliver paused again. "That is all I have to say about the matter."

Deborah Tolliver did not forgive Jesse. She blamed him for Karl's death, and from that point on she did not welcome

Jesse into the big house. Missy avoided him for several weeks, but late one afternoon he saw her sitting on a bench admiring the azaleas and flowers freshened by a morning shower. Jesse approached the bleached wood bench. "May I sit a spell with you?"

"If you want to."

They both stared at the flowers for several minutes, neither speaking until Jesse broke the silence. "I am truly sorry for your troubles."

After pondering his words, Missy replied. "What happened is not your fault. It is Karl's fault. He should have listened to you." She hesitated for a moment. "But Karl refused to listen to anybody."

"I believe your mother blames me."

"Right now mama blames everybody. She stays in her bedroom, sick with the vapors. I hate to speak ill of my brother, but mama never admitted Karl's flaws. Daddy lived with them for mama's sake, but Karl embarrassed him. Daddy tried to turn him into someone he could never be. It made both of them very unhappy."

"Well, sometimes we do not turn out to be the man we wanted to be. That is hard to live with. I can assure you of that."

"I guess. I went to New Orleans to get away from it all. Auntie and I went on to Charleston, Savannah, and Atlanta, but I could not leave the bad memories behind. So I came back, as lost as when I left."

After a long pause and reflection, Jesse turned to her and spoke softly. "A wise man once told me that it is not important how far you travel, it is what you bring back with you."

The conversation stopped there, but in the days ahead they sat on the bench at sunset to enjoy the wonderful view and talk about matters large and small. As weeks passed it became a romance and eventually an understanding that they would marry. Both would do that without great passion, but to ease their loneliness and carry on the family legacy. Tolliver promoted the arrangement for business purposes and his belief that Missy was second-hand property. He recognized Jesse's intelligence, his knowledge of family business affairs, and ruthlessness gained through many years of Tolliver's tutelage. Though he lacked a pedigree, Jesse became the best available option. Missy arranged a meeting between Jesse and her parents to acquire approval of the match, but Deborah Tolliver remained in her room with a headache. Displaying feigned cheerfulness the planter welcomed him into the family.

Missy had a condition. "I just have one request. I want a small wedding in the garden. Just me, Jesse, and family." She quickly added, "And a preacher. We can't forget him," she said with a giggle. Missy turned to Jesse. "Do you want to invite your family?"

"No. I have no one to invite." This irritated Tolliver, since the event could not be used to learn about Jesse's past. But having plowed that ground before with no success the old man remained silent.

Everyone agreed, and the meeting ended with Missy's demure kiss on Jesse's cheek. The next day she began moving the young man's personal items from his slender shotgun house into a large room in the big house far from her mother's quarters. During Jesse's courtship he had on some occasions gently pressed Missy for intimate caresses. She declined, playing the southern belle card learned from her mother and female friends and relatives. Missy teased him with hints about how pleased he would be after the wedding. "Don't be in a hurry," she often told him. "Everything will be wonderful." Though an experienced gambler, Jesse folded on her bluff.

Their wedding day turned sunny and mild, perfect for a garden nuptial. Missy looked beautiful in an almost-white gown. Tolliver wore a tuxedo that had not been let out to fit his enlarging paunch. Deborah Tolliver dressed for a funeral, and to her it was. The preacher, hand-picked by Tolliver, gave a short sermon and declared them husband and wife. After this brief ceremony the family walked to the big house for a glass of champagne and probably the chilliest, smallest, and shortest wedding reception in Delta history.

Jesse and his bride retired to their ornate quarters, and as Missy stripped to her shimmy, Jesse's appetite expanded. She still had a May-dew complexion and ample body, but the groom soon learned that what he considered wonderful possibilities, she considered objectionable behavior. Missy expressed surprise that he could have misunderstood her so profoundly. After his bride fell asleep, Jesse sat in bed and studied his surroundings. He knew that despite his experience he had been out played. The groom regretted that his marriage meant the end of a daydream in which Jesse ran away from the horrors of River Run, away from this southern torture chamber. Jesse had banked a substantial portion of his earnings. When depressed and guilt ridden, he fantasized about cashing out and catching a train to St. Louis and heading west, searching for redemption. This dream ended at the altar that day. Jesse admired the enormous bedroom, which opened into a sitting room with a set of Victorian chairs in front of a fireplace. Their four-poster bed of dark-stained wood held a mattress puffed up with feather comforters. Two chifferobes made with the same wood anchored opposite walls. Papered with a variety of pastoral scenes, the room had a comforting feel to it. When Jesse's attention returned to the fireplace he observed that the chairs were covered in red velvet. He smiled, recalling his primitive sexual awakening with Loretta in the New Orleans brothel, and he realized why some men prefer whores.

15

Tolliver's grandson arrived about 12 months later. Missy had walked into the gin office and sat down with a sigh.

"What is this about?" Jesse asked.

"I'm carrying your son inside me."

Jesse stood. "Are you sure?"

"Yes. Mama took me to our doctor in Memphis, and he confirmed it. I am saying it is a boy because I feel like it is. Don't ask me how, but I know it. I should have told you before, but I was unsure how you would react."

"What do you mean how I would react. I am delighted." Jesse gave Missy a long, comforting hug, but sensed there was more to the story, and there was. "How many months to go, give or take?"

"About seven months, give or take." Missy hesitated for a moment. "There are some things we need to talk about."

"What things?"

Missy fidgeted in the chair, a sure tell that what she planned to say might cause a row. "Mama and I talked about it on the drive home from Memphis. She wants to turn the sitting room beside her bedroom into a nursery. Marceline's granddaughter Precious would make an excellent nanny, and mama could keep a close eye on them. She is telling daddy about it now."

"By telling daddy do you mean that she is telling your father that she will do it or that she plans to do it. There is a big difference."

Missy became a little testy. "She knows how busy you are and that at my age I need a lot of recuperation. She is doing us a favor."

Jesse hesitated, then plunged ahead. "Very well then, I will tell you this with the bark off. Your mother hates my guts. She has always blamed me for Karl's death, though I do not know why. Before that she treated me like white trash because I did not come from an aristocratic Delta family. Now she wants to take my child."

Missy's discomfort became more obvious. "That is not fair. Nothing has been decided yet. I told her that we have to agree about it."

"And you are for it?"

"I am for trying it. If it does not work we can try something else."

Missy's pout signaled an end to the exchange. Jesse concluded that the family had already joined ranks so he decided to back off. "Do what you want."

This abrupt response surprised Missy. "Are you alright with it, or are you just saying that."

"I am just saying that to avoid a huge row. Besides, the vote is clearly three to one, so I lose. Who knows, maybe it will work out."

In naming the son, everyone contributed something. Deborah Tolliver insisted on Karl as a first name. Her husband required that Tolliver be the middle name. Missy and Jesse put Brody on the birth certificate. Tolliver attempted to use the event to pry a complete name out of Jesse, but that failed when Jesse ignored him. The leverage between them had shifted since Jesse now ran the empire as Tolliver's health declined, and Jesse had given him an heir. When the baby came home, Deborah Tolliver moved him into her living space where Jesse was not welcome. During the child's first few years Missy would bring his son to visit Jesse briefly on convenient afternoons. That ended at the start of the 1927 flood, when Deborah Tolliver moved to Memphis and took Karl with her. She used the flood's unhealthy consequences as an excuse, but Jesse knew that she had elected to live apart from two men she loathed. Missy would not discuss her mother's decision and began to stay in their Memphis townhouse much of the time. Jesse often felt like he had fathered a son and immediately put him up for adoption.

Following continuous deluges that spring the Mississippi River and its tributaries flooded the Arkansas Delta. One afternoon Tolliver walked into the gin office and sat down on a couch. "What are we going to do now?" he asked Jesse.

The young man looked up from the Memphis *Commercial Appeal*. "Listen to this," he said to Tolliver and began to summarize coverage. "Water has covered about 26,000 square miles in seven states. More than 930,000 persons are feeling the disastrous effects. This report says that many levees can no longer hold back Delta rivers and have collapsed." Jesse continued. "Water has poured through breaches and flooded vast stretches of farmland. Residents living along rivers have been warned to evacuate."

Jesse looked at Tolliver. "I intend to have our drivers transport white women and children to high ground along the ridge. I told Cross and his riding bosses to set up tents on our levees for the negroes. We need them to help maintain the levees. They will be more inclined to do that if their family's lives depend on it." They piled thousands of bags filled with dirt to strengthen levees. Still, sometimes water tore through earthen barriers, sweeping away everything in its path, including people.

One rainy morning Jesse drove his truck along a wide levee road to observe progress. He came upon Cross, who Jesse knew had become too old and infirm to manage the other riding bosses. Jesse had decided to replace him after the flooding ended. "How are we going to save anything if this continues?" he asked Cross.

"We need more help. I sent two men to the colored camps to get some boys. They're young, but they can fill sandbags. We'll have to use more of them." Jesse interrupted. "Mr. Tolliver called the Memphis mayor, and he said the cops over there would round up every negro on the streets and ship them across while the bridge is still holding. I expect them in the morning. The mayor said they will empty Beale Street if we need him to. The city is so high on the bluffs that they are not in any danger." Jesse knew of this arrangement since he and Tolliver had discussed how much to give the mayor in a campaign contribution.

As the business manager drove down a muddy road he saw riding bosses force black men to levees that might collapse at any minute. If workers hesitated they were pistol whipped and herded onto the soggy levees. After Jesse related this to Tolliver the planter interrupted and opened several newspapers he carried into the office.

"Have you seen these goddamn papers? I had Emmet get them for me in Memphis at the train station. Tolliver held up a copy of the *Chicago Defender*. "Look at these headlines. 'Refugees Herded Like Cattle to Stop Escape from Peonage. And Deny Food to Flood Sufferers. Work or Starve Rule.'" The planter sputtered. "What the hell do these people expect us to do? We got to do something." Tolliver held up a copy of the *Houston Informer*. "This paper says negro men are being kept in virtual slavery in the refugee camps by armed men at the behest of plantation owners and demagogic politicians. It says the politicians are in the hands of white planters. Negroes are being held in a vicious type of slavery. I told Gaylon to throw away any negro newspaper that comes to the post office. Every damn one of them. These outside troublemakers do not know the fix we are in and what we have to do to get out of it." Tolliver pitched the newspapers into a trash can. "What do we do now?" he asked Jesse.

"No matter what we do, we will probably miss a crop this year or plant late and have reduced yields so I think we work a different angle. We put pressure on our political allies to provide generous federal disaster aid. If we get cash to replace crop income we can come out way ahead. That money will go straight to the bottom line. We will not need most of our day labor except for a few hands we decide to keep. They can help our tenants improve rented land to ready it for production. Almost all of our fences are down. They can fix them. We continue to furnish everyone from our store. Their accounts will be too big to pay off, so we can offset next year's rent as well. If we play this right we can turn a loss into a win."

Tolliver nodded. "I expect you to take care of that. You let me know when I need to lean on our politicians. We have put boodle in their pockets for a long time and asked very little of them. They can damn well pay us back now." Jesse put the plan in play, and Tolliver muscled the politicians into turning on the money spigot.

Due to Tolliver's deteriorating health, Jesse had assumed virtually all the plantation management responsibilities. This helped him justify his parental abdication. Late that summer Missy arranged to have a rare family brunch at Paulette's in Memphis when Karl came home from the South Carolina military school he attended. Jesse was stunned at how much his son had grown, physically and intellectually, since their last meeting. He accepted a stiff, formal hug from the boy. Jesse assumed, correctly as it turned out, that Deborah Tolliver had poisoned the well that both father and son had to drink from. During the meal Jesse received an account from Karl about his excellent progress among scions of prominent southern families. The brunch had a stilted quality that made all of them uncomfortable, and when it ended they seemed relieved. It became typical of family events that brought them together.

Jesse and Missy stayed the night in their large suite at the Peabody Hotel with an expansive view of the river. As he looked out a window early the next morning Jesse could see over the tops of buildings to the piers and the faces of ghosts that haunted the river. Now the wharves were filled with barges lashed together, waiting to be pushed upriver by diesel tugs. The glorious riverboat days had passed into history. But what days they were, he thought. Regret about this loss brought into focus the Colonel and all the characters Jesse met during his apprenticeship. It reminded him of the many times he sat on a texas deck guard while the boat swayed gently at a pier and stevedores pushed dollies carrying cotton bales onto the main deck. That reflection became a determination to find out more about the Colonel and, if possible, learn what happened to him. Why this became so important at that moment Jesse could not say. Perhaps he hoped it would somehow connect him to a past that had promised him a good life, even though he turned it down. Maybe memories would help explain his decision. Whatever the reason, he vowed to see it through. The next afternoon he called his personal attorney from the gin office. The secretary put him through immediately. "Hello, Jesse. What can I do for you?" Dennis Brady asked with his deep courtroom voice."

"I need to find somebody."

"Who do you need to find? Or do I want to know."

"Nothing nefarious. An old friend that I have not seen in decades. I want to know what happened to him. Who do you know that finds people?"

"We use Roger Thompson for our divorce investigations. He usually finds people sleeping in the wrong bed, but I think he finds other people as well. He has an office here in Memphis."

"Can you give me his phone number?"

"Sure, hold for a minute." Brady thumbed through his address book and soon returned to the line with the number. Jesse thanked him, and Brady added, "I assume you remember that the partners and I need to borrow your duck blind when the season opens."

"Yes. I'll have it ready."

"Say hello to Missy for me."

"Will do, and thanks, Dennis."

Jesse called the number, and a secretary picked up with news that Thompson was out of town. She agreed to have him call Jesse the next day. After that Jesse settled in to recall everything he knew that might prove useful to the investigator and soon realized how little he knew about his mentor.

When Thompson called he seemed transparent for a man holding so many secrets. "Dennis said that you need some help finding a person."

"That is correct."

"Is this person involved in illegal activities?"

Jesse smiled and almost laughed. "I haven't seen him in more than 30 years, so he is most certainly dead and therefore not involved in any such activities."

"Do you have any information about him that will help me get started?"

"Some, but it is old. I can tell you what I know when we meet. If you are wasting your time and my money just tell me. I will pay you for the visit, and we will part ways."

"If I take this assignment my $200 per week fees are due on Fridays along with expenses. I will give you receipts for them. In addition, I charge a $200 finder's fee if I am successful. I require a one-week advance." He paused for a reaction.

"Your fee will not be a problem."

They met the next day in Jesse's gin office. When Thompson walked in Jesse read him fast. He had a thin, ascetic face, a slender frame and confident movements. His light brown hair was cut short in crew style. Jesse assumed he had military experience and most likely lived a spartan life. All these ideas merged almost instantly, and Jesse would bet a 40-acre farm that they were accurate or real close.

Jesse rose from his plush leather office chair and held out his hand. "Good of you to come."

"Thanks for asking."

They sat down, and Jesse began his story. "You may find this hard to believe, but it is all true."

Thompson smiled. "A lot of what I hear is hard to believe, but true."

Jesse smiled back. "I'll start at the beginning. Everyone called him the Colonel, but I do not know why." The private investigator pulled out a narrow notebook and made copious entries. He asked only the right questions, those that might be helpful in his search. In replying, Jesse often backtracked and elaborated. He occasionally looked up at an antique clock on a shelf and stopped talking at the two-hour mark. "I need to take a break. This is exhausting. May I offer you a cup of coffee?"

"Thanks, but no. I have what I need to start. There is enough material here to follow most of the typical leads. If I am to begin I need my retainer."

Jesse wrote out the check. "How will I reach you if I remember anything else or need to pay your weekly fee?"

"Call my secretary and leave a message. I check in with her regularly. She will set our appointments and take care of other matters." Thompson stood to accept the check, thanked Jesse, and walked out the door. He had wasted not one word nor one minute, and Jesse knew right away that he had hired the right man.

One week later Thompson's secretary called to delay their first meeting for a week. She said that Thompson had nothing substantial to report at that time and would collect his fee at the next meeting. That following week the secretary called again with the same message. She declined to comment about the status of his investigation and made clear that Thompson alone handled such matters.

A week later Thompson called to schedule an appointment. "Do you have anything?" Jesse asked during the phone call.

"Yes. We can talk about it tomorrow afternoon if that is convenient."

Jesse struggled a bit with his apprehension while waiting in his office. He had become skeptical about finding out anything useful.

After he and Thompson sat down, the investigator astonished him. "I think I found your man. Take a look at this photocopy and tell me if this is your Colonel."

Jesse took the copy and saw the Colonel staring back at him. Though a young man in the photo, it was the Colonel. He experienced an emotional rush and struggled to tamp down his enthusiasm. "It is him, for sure. How did you find him?"

Thompson opened a file folder and pulled out several typed pages. "He is buried in Wilmington, Delaware, and was originally from there. Some family members still live in Wilmington. I found a niece, and she let me photograph the original photo. The lady is sort of a family historian and knows what little there is to know about him."

"What was his name?"

"Hilliard Simmons. I talked with her for a while, and the history tracks."

"Very well, but how on earth did you find him?"

"Eventually by his clothes, after exhausting several lines of inquiry. The man you described would wear only bespoke suits of the highest quality. Your description suggested materials mostly for southern weather, so custom made suits from Memphis or New Orleans were likely. I started in Memphis but found no leads there or at cities downriver. In New Orleans only the Steinberg family tailors on Canal Street go back that far. Augustus Steinberg was dead, but his son Arthur inherited the business. Though a child at the time, Arthur was a cutter in his father's shop and remembered a meticulous client called the Colonel. The man impressed the boy through his manners and comportment. Though apparently wealthy, he lacked a planter's arrogance and gambler's extravagance. He also recalled his father mentioning that the Colonel was from Wilmington, Delaware. That led me there, and I found several prominent relatives after a search. Most knew that he had become a professional gambler, but not much else about him. The niece is in poor health, but she is cogent, and I believe her information is reliable. The family learned of Mr. Simmons' death from his wife in Louisiana. She called to alert them that he had requested to be buried in one of his family's Wilmington cemetery plots. So she shipped the body to Delaware. Mr. Simmons' wife told the niece that they married late in life and lived on her plantation. One of the peculiar things about the story is that the widow sent a valuable diamond ring to be buried with the body, but none of his relatives know why. The widow provided very little personal information and asked not to be contacted.

"Mr. Simmons was buried in a family plot at the Catholic cemetery with a small marker containing nothing but his name."

"Tell me anything else that you found out about him."

Thompson shuffled through his papers. "His father was a well-respected surgeon in the region. His mother was from one of Wilmington's most prosperous families. Mr. Simmons had two sisters. Both are dead. His father prepared him for a medical profession, and as a boy he appeared to be precocious. The niece had been told that while his friends played baseball, Mr. Simmons stayed in his room reading history.

He graduated from a Catholic school when he was 15 and went to Yale to prepare for medical school. Something happened in his third year to change his mind. He did not enroll for the final year, and his father, who apparently was a bully, went to the campus to find out what had gone wrong with his son. The niece heard that when his father returned the only thing he had to say was that his son had acquired an unfortunate gambling habit and dropped out of school. The father made it clear that he had given up on him. Apparently no one in the family saw him after he left for Yale, except for a cousin. She claimed to have seen someone who strongly resembled Mr. Simmons in the lobby of the Palmer House hotel in Chicago. The cousin said he was wearing a military uniform, but she did not talk to him since he appeared to be in a rush to leave with several well-dressed gentlemen. Beyond that the trail is cold until you met him on that steamboat."

Both men remained quiet for a minute or two before Jesse spoke. "You are good at your job."

"Thompson nodded. "Thank you. Do you want me to pursue this further? I hesitate to do that because it would be exorbitantly expensive, and I doubt if I can turn up anything beyond what you already know."

"No. You found what I wanted to know." Jesse pulled out his checkbook, and they settled up. After shaking hands, Thompson handed him the file and went on his way.

16

Jesse reflected on his two mentors, the Colonel and Tolliver, and how different they were. Technically, the Colonel could be considered dishonest, but he had charm, elegance, an impressive intelligence and a somewhat admirable code that he adhered to. Tolliver lacked any redeeming qualities. He also had little time left to live. The planter's declining health had become increasingly obvious and trips to Baptist Hospital in Memphis more frequent. Late one afternoon, as Jesse searched for a book in the family library that he had not read, the elderly planter walked in slowly. "I thought you already read all these books."

"Not yet, but close to it." Jesse grew silent, hoping that the old man would go away. Since he had taken charge of all

Tolliver's business, Jesse had become increasingly intolerant of the dying man.

Tolliver pressed ahead. "The doctors said yesterday that I am dying faster than they thought I would. They want me to start taking some godawful treatment that hurts like hell and may or may not work. I told them that the juice ain't worth the squeeze. I am ready to move on to whatever comes next." Tolliver hesitated, perhaps thinking that Jesse would say something comforting, but his son-in-law had nothing comforting to say. "What are you doing tomorrow morning?"

This question struck Jesse as odd, since Tolliver had always ignored his plans and demanded that Jesse tend to whatever Tolliver wanted him to do. "I do not have anything scheduled," Jesse replied.

"I want one more trip around the place."

Jesse reluctantly agreed to join him, and the next morning Jesse drove them slowly around the plantation in Tollliver's Cadillac. They stared out the car window in silence at black, flat earth too wet to work. Farmers had parked their red and green tractors on muddy turn rows. The rain had done its damage and moved on, leaving an indifferent blue sky and mild temperature. It would be the old man's last survey of his empire.

Tolliver died along with the stock market in October of that year. A maid found the planter when she entered his bedroom with a carafe of coffee and two scratch biscuits covered with cream gravy. Missy and her mother elected to have only a secular graveside service since Tolliver worshiped worldly power, not God. While standing beside Missy near a large mound of black dirt from the gravesite it occurred to Jesse that Tolliver had chosen to die at a good time. Economic affairs throughout America had become chaotic and treacherous, and now the burden of protecting the family's interests fell entirely on his shoulders.

Jesse no longer cared that Deborah Tolliver had turned Karl into a stranger and that she benefited from his financial acumen. And he lacked compassion while watching her slowly waste away. Her skin looked like pale parchment stretched over a skeleton. She had become addicted to sedatives, and two years after her husband's death she took too many. Missy called it a mistake, as did their family doctor, but Jesse believed otherwise.

17

Jesse carefully followed the Depression's consequences by reading several newspapers every day and keeping a sharp eye on the plantation ledger. More than 60 Arkansas banks closed in November, and 46 soon followed. River Run tenants made crop loans each year to pay production expenses, but after banks went under, farmers went with them. The plantation could not fund production loans for all its tenants, so Jesse kept the best producers and ran off the others. As had been his habit for many years, he found opportunity in the evolving disaster. After Jesse helped establish an organization with powerful regional planters they appointed him to represent them.

He helped lobby congress for a massive aid program and got it. The Agricultural Adjustment Act required the federal government to pay farmers not to plant crops. In theory this would reduce supply and increase prices. Planters insisted that cash payments be routed through them. They were supposed to share the money with their tenants, but most did not. The program called for landlords to avoid terminating tenant contracts, but with planted acres reduced, landlords had no need for many tenants and let them go. Hundreds of dispossessed families roamed country roads searching for their next meal.

Planters faced few risks as they corrupted the federal program, but sometimes problems surfaced unexpectedly. Jesse became the person who handled them for regional landlords though he disliked the aggravation. One morning he took a phone call from Fletcher Norvell, a Mississippi County planter and business associate. "Jesse, we need to talk about something that has developed and might cause us problems."

"What is it?"

"I just took a call from Congressman Stabler. It seems that a do-gooder in Memphis told him about program abuses in our area. He wants to come here and see for himself what happened to people we let go. I stalled him until Monday."

"Well, drive him around in circles until you run out of gas."

"That's what I usually do, but someone has been sneaking around and gave him a list of locations to check. He told me that he wanted to be driven to those places. I told the congressman that I would send a driver to Osceola this afternoon to pick up his list. I need you to come with me and let's see what he's talking about."

"When you get the list call me, and I will drive over there. Make sure you know where we are going. I do not want to drive around lost all afternoon." The phone call increased Jesse's irritation. He had been dealing all morning with reports of a tenant farmers union being organized in Tyronza, a small Poinsett County town. Jesse sent one of his riding bosses, Hershel Smith, to a plantation near the town to find out what a friendly landlord had to say. Jesse took an early lunch alone in the big house while he waited for Smith. He offered his manager a bowl of peach cobbler when Smith walked in. As usual, the short, muscular man had a face painted red by the sun.

Smith declined the cobbler and immediately reported what he learned about the union. "A bunch of tenants and farm workers got riled up by a guy named Mitchell who runs a dry-cleaning business and Clay East, who is city marshal and owns a gas station."

"Why are the two of them interfering in our business?"

"They are socialists and admit it."

Jesse had been chasing the last bite of vanilla ice cream around the bowl with his spoon to mix it with a bit of cobbler but stopped abruptly. "Are you sure they are socialists or is that just a rumor."

"No. It's true. The planters I talked to say the two make no bones about it."

Jesse finished his final bite and pushed the bowl aside. "What do we know about the union?"

"They say it's got white folks and negroes and even women in it."

"You are sure it has both races and women?"

"That's what everyone says. Landlords are already gathering their names and where they live. They plan to nip it in the bud."

This posed a serious problem, which Jesse recognized immediately. Playing off one race against another had long been a successful planter tactic when busting up a union. With that opportunity lost, more intimidation and force might be necessary. But Jesse decided to deal with that crisis after helping Norvell with his problem.

The first place they drove to had a family of four living in a hovel about ten feet wide and 20 feet long, made of corrugated tin and scraps of lumber. It had a dirt floor and only two small openings in the sides. The husband, wife and three children stood in front of the wretched structure and stared at Norvell, who had driven Jesse to the location.

Jesse also stared at Norvell. "Fletcher, you cannot have the congressman looking at white people living like this. He may start a congressional enquiry, and we must avoid that. Next thing you know we will have northern politicians and newspapers howling. Have your men bring some two by fours and tin sheets out here and fix this place up. Bring some food and a cooking pot, better clothes, too."

Norvell objected. "These people aren't my tenants anymore. I let them go. I'm laying out what they were farming for my government money."

"I know that Fletcher, but we promised not to do that. We had to in order to get that money. We have to do whatever it takes to keep that money coming our way. Do not lose sight of the big picture." Jesse paused, irritated by Norvell's inability to understand the political and possibly public relations consequences of this scene. He also dreaded riding up and down country roads looking at the squalid existence of tenant families illegally dislocated to gain planters more government money. He turned to his friend. "Do all of these places on the list look like this?"

"Pretty much, but I don't have any responsibility for these people. They don't belong to me anymore."

"That is not the point. We have to make sure that the congressman goes away satisfied."

Norvell bit off a chew from his plug and thought about the situation. "What if these people want to know why we're doing this now?"

"Tell them you've been planning all along to help everybody but are just now getting around to it. Make sure you are standing beside the congressman while he talks to them. That will keep them from saying things we do not want them to say. They will be afraid to lose what little they have."

Norvell complied but didn't like it one bit.

18

As dreary years crept by during the 1930s the desperation of tenant farmers and day laborers intensified. Led by Jesse, regional planters managed to strangle most opposition, but the Southern Tenant Farmers Union maintained constant pressure on them. The union called for strikes, issued press releases about landlord brutality and exposed their manipulation of federal programs. Planters sent riding bosses to threaten and beat union members and disrupt their meetings by firing into churches, their usual gathering places. Tent colonies of displaced farm workers sprouted up around the region and garnered newspaper and magazine coverage. The omnipresent misery led to a confrontation between Jesse and Missy that had been a long time coming.

Missy started it one evening at dinner. "I was taking Mazie to her sister's house this afternoon on that dirt road by the Carver place. Some white people were walking down the road toward us. It was a mother and two little boys. The boys had two puppies in their arms, and the mother was holding a chicken. I suppose that was to be their supper. The father was a little bit behind them. He had been beaten up pretty bad. I had Russell stop the car, and I asked the man who beat him up. He said a deputy sheriff did it after accusing him of stealing an egg. One egg, Jesse. These are white people. I think what is happening to them is wrong, and somebody ought to be punished for it."

Usually Jesse ignored Missy's rare bouts of concern for poor people. During their many years together, he had become uninterested in anything she had to say. But the pressure he endured while attempting to protect the Tolliver empire and his withering health made him unwilling to pretend. Her lament triggered an explosive reaction. He turned to her and vented his anger. "You may not be aware of it, but one night many years ago I boarded your steamer in Memphis to follow you and Karl across the river. There was a string of shackled black men on board falsely convicted of vagrancy. That is how I ended up in the swamp and how I got typhus. When we made it to the convict work camp with the prisoners, I realized that the new men were there to replace seriously ill and dying men. They were treated with a barbarity that I will not share with you because it is utterly disgusting." Missy stared at a large portrait of her father on the wall while Jesse continued.

"Those men and hundreds of others, black and white, have been abused and murdered by your family .... and me, god help me, after I became an enforcer in this criminal enterprise. Corruption is how you maintain your expensive Memphis wardrobe. That is what paid Karl's gambling debts. It is how your family affords its mansion in New Orleans. It maintains this plantation and pays the poor people who allow you to live in great luxury without lifting a finger. It provides a thousand other things that are considered by wealthy southerners to be their birthright." Missy flushed as he continued. "Slavery never ended here, it just took on new forms and new names. You need to be honest with yourself and admit it. I'm too old and ill to pretend differently. When I look in a mirror, I see someone who once was a good man, but not anymore. I realize that like your father, I too am a monster."

Missy rose quickly and threw her linen napkin on the table. "I am going to my bedroom. You should find somewhere else to sleep." Jesse looked up at the oil painting of Tolliver on the dining room wall, then to that of Missy's brother Karl hung beside it. Jesse recalled the day he held Karl's head underwater until all that remained were large bubbles and the sight of his wide, terrified eyes.

About a week later Missy moved to New York to be near their son. After Harvard, Karl practiced law at one of the large New York firms and never returned to River Run. This was in large part because of Jesse. For many years his son had shared a townhouse with a man that Karl called a close friend. Jesse recognized that the man also was Karl's lover, and he considered their relationship a disgusting perversion. The complete separation between father and son began when Karl once mentioned to his mother that he would return on Christmas and bring the man he called his partner. Jesse refused, insisting that Karl come alone. As a result, Karl never returned home. Though not entirely comfortable with Karl's arrangement, Missy accepted what she could not change. Jesse could not change what he would not accept.

A brief rapprochement occurred after Jesse's stroke and the onset of seizures. Missy learned of his deteriorating health from their family lawyer, who recommended that she and Karl come to Memphis and discuss the estate plan. They did, and due to a residual scrap of loyalty to Jesse she insisted that they visit him. Both were shocked by what they found. Marceline's granddaughters, Precious and Beloved, cared for Jesse and helped him into the study where his wife and son waited. He could only string together sentences if he spoke slowly and concentrated intensely. Jesse told Karl between labored breaths that he wanted most of all to visit the old plantation landing.

"Okay, we can do that," Karl said. "I have not been there since I was a kid." Karl drove his father to the place, and after they arrived he helped Jesse into a wheelchair and pushed him to what little remained of the old dock. Most of the aged, rotting wood had been claimed by the river, which that day was lower than normal due to a drought. Jesse looked down at the residue and recalled his arrival there a lifetime ago. He wanted Karl to know his story and brought with him hundreds of typed pages in a binder that contained honest and complete recollections. Jesse handed it to Karl and asked him not to open it until after his father's death. As Jesse stared at the river he began to cry quietly.

Karl was stunned by his self-contained, stoic father's breakdown and awkwardly put his hand on Jesse's shoulder. "Dad, I do not know what is wrong, but can I help?"

Jesse wiped away tears with his fingers. "Nothing you can do, Karl. All the things I have done I own. I became one of them. Lost my way, and it is too late to turn back."

Their journey ended there, and they returned in silence to the big house where Missy waited for them. Before entering, Jesse looked up at the cloudy sky and observed a string of geese playing follow the leader in their v formations. They might be bound for heaven, Jesse thought, but he was not. Jesse lived his final days in terror, fearing that Old Scratch was waiting for him.

NOTES ON SOURCES

Three primary resources helped in writing this novel:

Steamboat history and culture from my book, *Smoke Up the River. Steamboats and the Arkansas Delta.*

Riverboat gambling from George H. Devol's *Forty Years A Gambler on The Mississippi.*

Plantation life in the Delta from another book I authored, *Moaning Low. From* Slavery *to Peonage. Involuntary Servitude in the Arkansas Delta.*